EVERYTHING IS BORROWED

Also by Nathaniel Popkin

FICTION

Lion and Leopard

NONFICTION

Song of the City

The Possible City

Philadelphia: Finding the Hidden City
(with Joseph E. B. Elliott and Peter Woodall)

Who Will Speak for America?
(edited with Stephanie Feldman)

To Maxine —
A very favorite reader!

EVERYTHING
IS BORROWED

a novel

NATHANIEL POPKIN

Sept 2 2018

NEW DOOR BOOKS
Philadelphia 2018

New Door Books
An imprint of P. M. Gordon Associates, Inc.
2115 Wallace Street
Philadelphia, Pennsylvania 19130
U.S.A.

This is a work of fiction. Any resemblance herein to actual persons,
living or dead, or to actual events or locales is purely coincidental.

Library of Congress Control Number: 2017916208
ISBN 978-0-9995501-1-3

To Peter S.,
for patience, honesty, and wisdom

Ideality and reality therefore collide—in what medium? In time? That is indeed an impossibility. In what, then? In eternity? That is indeed an impossibility. In what, then? In consciousness—there is the contradiction.

Søren Kierkegaard, unpublished draft, *Johannes Climacus, or De omnibus dubitandum est*

Credit where credit is due, but apart from the heavens and world history, there is still a history called the individual's history.

Constantin Constantius, "An Open Letter to Professor Heiberg, Knight of Daneborg"

1

I LIKE TO SEE THINGS for myself, to enter a space as if taking hold of it, to note the contours, the dimensions, the volume, and only then can I imagine what might be. It should be obvious: the architect is to immerse himself in place. His building should emerge from the ground as if it had grown there, as if it couldn't be found anywhere else, as if nothing else could fill the space.

It must have been during the last few years I spent at Clarkson Architects, by then a senior associate, that this way of thinking led me to consider how I would approach my own commissions, in my own firm. Now I sit at the computer in my office, my back to the window, and someone's upstairs flush whispers down the stack pipe in the corner.

The site I'm working on, a parking lot, is on the computer screen. A man younger than I am wants to build an apartment house there. In exactly a month, this man, Armen Terzian, will present my conceptual plans to the people who live in that part of the city, an old, densely populated section near the Delaware. The developer is lucky: an empty site of this scale—more than a half-block long—is hard to find.

The neighbors will be able to vote, yea or nay, whether they approve of the proposal.

My associate, Nadia Chamoun, sits at a table in our outer studio. Nadia has been with me a little longer than a year. She is preparing a report on solar and wind conditions at the site while I evaluate various alternative massings. Terzian has told us the apartment house must be five stories, taller than is allowed. When I suggested we could fit his desired number of apartments in a four-story building, he told me not to worry. "Design it at five. I suppose we'll sue if we have to."

I haven't done much with the massings. Hoping to buy some time, I've tried to conceal this from Nadia. But she sees through me. Maybe the creative block, if that's what it is, comes from Terzian. What kind of man is he? He calls here once a week. Maybe he, too, is on to me or maybe he just likes the sound of Nadia's voice. I should go to the parking lot; I should immerse myself.

I urge myself over to the bank of five windows that, facing south, look out on Locust Street. I must have put the shades down earlier, but I can tell the light, as evening approaches, has begun to sharpen. I open the right shade to the slender young plane tree imprisoned in its sidewalk pit, learning to be impassive against the heat. The poor unwavering tree holding in its thirst. But the bark of the plane tree detaches itself in scales, as if the tree is plagued by stress. The desiccating leaves take on the appearance of tanned leather or papery filo and they dissolve under foot.

Three volunteers for a group called Tree Tenders planted the plane tree the same Saturday four years ago when a realtor handed me the keys to this office, on the second floor of this shabby building. After eighteen years with other people's firms, at last I was on my own (and free of a constipated marriage, too). I took the cheapest two-room office on the nicest block, near Rittenhouse Square. (The block is filled almost uniformly with three- and four-story row houses of various architectural styles, many with handsome storefront windows and fanciful details—all but mine, with its drab mid-century façade.) I shook the realtor's hand and went upstairs. Drawn to the bank of windows across the second floor, I stood here, in this same spot, and watched the three volunteers lift the tree into the pit. One of them looked up, red-faced, as he grimaced and tried to straighten the tree, a look of moral confusion. He must have realized the pit was too small for the tree.

I think back to that first day, a moment suspended in assurance. Three commissions in hand, including the redesign of an entire shopping street that would bring my firm widespread attention and an award, and many others I would sign on later. All of them would get from me an architecture of immersion. Immediately, in this room, I ripped out the ugly drop ceiling. The next day I repaired the cracks in the plaster; I painted everything white.

I walk from my office out into our main studio. Nadia is printing out wind diagrams. She has intense focus. "I will come back!" I say, but I'm not even sure she realizes I'm leaving.

I pass the Yogorino and go into Rittenhouse Square. Already I realize I've been walking too fast. The light is sharp but the air is dull and thick; this and the purple-green leaves of the high trees give the impression of entering a tropical forest.

Below, in the shade's edge by the service hut, a dark-haired woman is straddling a man, only his bare, bony feet and edge of his jeans in the light. She rocks slowly, almost imperceptibly, as if to guard against suspicion. Or simply due to the heat. The edge of her skirt drags slightly along the dust and grass and I recall Eva, somewhere in distant memory, Eva below me, on the ground.

I dip my hand in the reflection pool and stir the water hesitantly. It's too hot to walk to Terzian's parking lot. I unbutton the second button of my shirt. Across the square, I wait for the number 12 bus. The driver wears a rolled-up white towel on the back of his neck.

The surface of Terzian's parking lot is rough and ugly. Like a gash in the street, it exposes the membranes of the city. Light isn't supposed to penetrate into the interior of the block, and I imagine the scars can't be healed by sun. You aren't supposed to see the half-tumbling back garden walls of the buildings that ring the parking lot; the morning glories are meant to be private. You shouldn't see the broken skin caked with asphalt and caked over again, weeds rupturing the surface of the lot like the lesions of some inexorable disease. Except maybe it's beautiful: the chimney of a missing row house like a ghost or a memory, a pitched roof propped hesitantly in a horizon of straight lines, stucco below giving way. Now only the outline remains of an alley that must have run west from 4th Street into the center of the block. If I look at an old map, what will it be called? Bigelow? Or Constantine?

Why am I hesitant to cover all this up? According to my client, Armen Terzian, what he envisions is very simple: Thirty-five apartments and two retail stores, some social space for the tenants. A place for their bikes. An exercise room, a roof-top pool. Parking? But where will it go? Digging in my mind as I try to imagine the project before me, I also begin to dig through the layers of history. A city, like a person's life, collects like a delta.

I haven't spent much time in this neighborhood in years, despite its popularity. Once or twice perhaps to the crêperie Beau Monde, a meeting with a prospective client at the Famous Deli. Once, only last year, I caught an old friend's performance of electronic music at the little bookstore on 4th Street. We drank rye Old Fashioneds at Southwark, where the bartenders wear crisp white shirts.

Years ago, on Thursday nights, we would come down here and drink at a bar on a narrow, dark corner. In those days we drove, I don't know why. Because we couldn't afford taxis. In those days the subway ran twenty-four hours, but we never considered it. We always drove.

When we couldn't find a spot on the street, we paid three dollars and parked here, in this same lot.

The parking lot attendant comes over. He asks if I need any help. His voice is quiet, almost a whisper, and his eyes are searching and kind. "Can't find your car?" He is African or possibly Caribbean. He holds his hands together at his heart, the four fingers of the right hand between the left's thumb and index finger. A prayer grip. I don't want to tell him I'm going to obliterate his lot. The phrase "fill in the void" comes to mind—but the emptiness, too, is a volume filled with meaning. I shake my head instead. "Having a look," I say, finally. The asphalt is so hot it seems to swell under foot.

The buildings that line the parking lot on the western edge are on Passyunk Avenue. I walk around to it—mostly a charming row of shops, but I sense a haggardness, too, a place tired of itself. I wonder if the height of the apartment house could be pushed up even another story beyond Terzian's five stories on the interior of the site if I can maintain a three-story edge at the street. The spatial difference could be made up with a terrace at the fourth story. A picture of the terrace, with its greenery and tables, umbrellas and lounge chairs, comes to mind, and in that moment, with the sun lowering yet still far above the buildings, a fierce and lonely ache presses in behind my eyes. I recognize it, for nowadays I can see it coming from a far distance: a terrifying fear of my own impotence and unoriginality.

The creative block began well before the Terzian contract, in fact just after I won a prestigious award two years ago. Ready-made, without effort, I slide the stale vision of Terzian's apartment house into place. The more easily it fits, the more suddenly desperate I feel—a man tired of himself. His ideas are tired; his ambivalence is tiresome.

I return to the interior of the parking lot and drift toward the guard shack. *Platicar* is a Spanish word a colleague at Clarkson once taught me. Rodrigo Ramirez. "You have to chat up the client, the client's mother, the client's wife, the client's little dog," he said. "We have a word for it . . ." *Platicar, plati-cando* . . . an effortless word that settles so easily on the tongue. I wish to *platicar* the guard, to be close to him if for only a moment, somehow to compensate for the sterile state of my mind. But the guard isn't there. A cheap desk fan rocks back and forth inside the shack, letting out a tiny wail each time it turns.

The fan is perfectly illuminated, isolated in the sun's golden hour, as if in a vintage photograph of a backwater Southern county seat, or a tourist's gaze through a window of old Havana. I recall our old bar this way, a hidden jewel in a half-opened box. The memory of the colors of bottles on the shelf behind the bar reminds me now of a candy display in the old city of Jerusalem, in a dark souq strung with beads. The graffiti on the outside walls of the bar, and all the way down the alley, was like this too, when illuminated by the headlights of a car.

In ordinary light, the alley walls were dark and sad in those days, as if the vibrant color of the graffiti lines had been discolored by soot and filth, and also disappointment. Years later, watching the film *Mikey and Nicky*, I discovered these same streets again, barren and cold as they were in 1976, when the movie came out.

I leave the parking lot and turn east toward our old bar. I switch to the shady side of the street and back again. The corner that I am certain is where our bar used to be is now a restaurant, Kabobeesh. I've seen this same restaurant, with the same name and sign set in the same typeface, in West Philadelphia, where we lived in those days when we came all the way down here at night. The other Kabobeesh, at 42nd and Chestnut, a corner that always seemed forlorn and damaged, is in an old stainless steel diner car that has been completely hidden beneath stucco walls and cinderblock. Only the shape remains, trapped beneath the sharp lines of the new beige exterior, another ghost form of the street.

The Kabobeesh on Chestnut Street serves Indian and Pakistani food, at least as I recall. This Kabobeesh on 4th Street, in the storefront that was, in the old days, our favorite bar, serves Turkish food. "Turkish and Mediterranean cuisine," it says. On Chestnut Street, I have always thought "Indian" is intentionally misleading. Maybe the owners think no one will want Pakistani food because they won't know what it is. Sometimes the city is hard to read.

2

From the old bar, I walk a block and a half to Lombard Street to grab a taxi back to the office. A taxi will be quicker than the bus. But instead of taking the fastest route straight up Lombard and turning on 22nd to Locust Street, the driver turns on 13th, right into backed-up traffic. Eventually we make it to Walnut and turn left, but Walnut is even worse. Buses jam the right lane. The weather report plays on the little screen attached to the back side of the front seat. 95 degrees, 97, 94, 98 . . . I push the button off. "Listen!" I start to say when we finally reach Broad Street. I'll get out. I'll walk. But the driver doesn't hear me. The meter seems to accelerate. The seat feels slippery from sweat.

Ten minutes go by and we reach 16th Street, just two blocks further. That's enough. I fumble for my wallet, which drops to the floor of the taxi. Bills crumple in my clumsy hand. I try to stuff them back in the wallet, but they won't lie flat. "Please, sir, you can pay with a credit card," the driver says. "It's so much easier."

It's so much easier . . . Before the taxi pulls away, in the window's reflection I take notice of my hair pasted to my forehead, my shirt untucked, sleeves rolled haphazardly. I have to compose myself, smooth the wrinkles on my shirt and pants, straighten my belt . . . And there is Cecil Baxter when, finished the grooming and resettling, I look up. Dressed in a guayabera and linen slacks, he seems unaffected by the heat.

"Moscowitz! Come have a drink," he says.

Automatically I decline. Cecil demands too much. Since childhood, when we were six . . . I can't do it now. I have to get back to the office, to the Terzian account. "My associate, Nadia, is waiting."

He smiles, observing me. "One drink at the Happy Rooster, Nicholas. One drink. How are you? Are you OK?"

"I'm great, Cecil. Trying to figure something out."

He tries to guess. "You're trying to cantilever something. Architects are always cantilevering."

Now I observe him and wonder how he keeps up so well. He rarely sleeps. What does he do? Deals? Investments? It's never been clear. I've never wanted to know. He is intent on the drink. "One drink," I acquiesce. "I have to get back to the office before 7:30."

The Happy Rooster, with its Savoy air, is mostly empty. The usual customers are away at the beach. Only a few tourists, eating dinner too early, sit in the booths. We take the table for two in the window. "This is the only place where I can feel almost human," he says. "And it's perfectly all right to stare into the bosom of the waitress, if you like."

I try to avoid mentioning my crisis of confidence. I ask him about his mother, Adrienne, and her horses. One is white with gray spots, the other gray with white spots. He asks how it is to be single, "after all this time."

I shrug.

"You were always like this—nonplussed. But something is eating at you. I could tell the second I saw you frantically tucking in your shirt."

Cecil grew up in a sprawling, single-story modernist house, built in 1952, with an immense, closely clipped lawn a mile down the River Road from my house. His house was leaky and damp despite the large plate glass windows; mildew was like a badge of the aristocracy of Bucks County. Our mothers had been friends—Adrienne had even bought some of my mother's early artwork and Hilda, my mother, appreciated Adrienne's worldliness. In those days she was still seeking out Europhiles before giving up altogether and becoming a hippie. And Adrienne, who had studied Klimt at Wellesley, insisted that Cecil and his younger brother Edward grow up connected to nature. Until age eight they were allowed to run and play along the river naked; when I first saw him, Cecil and his uncircumcised self were bouncing across the back lawn, stick in hand to dig for worms.

"You remember when our mothers would go to lunch and we'd lie there naked, always naked, in the grass, and you would say something like, 'Why isn't there nothing, Cecil, not nothing, less than nothing, because nothing is something. Why not?'"

"What kind of kid . . . Did you answer? I hope you didn't try to answer."

"How could I answer? I would laugh, but I wouldn't try to grasp what you were saying. Giggle, I think."

"Should have knocked me upside the head."

"Work is good? Any girlfriends?"

"No time, really."

"And you're staying in the big house on Aspen Street? Ever thought of moving?"

"I haven't had time to think about it."

"It's a beautiful house, of course."

I notice his hands, his fingers, still smooth, still a young man's. He's almost finished with his gin and tonic. I've barely touched my glass of white wine. It's too sweet. Nadia might be leaving the office . . .

"Have you ever thought about giving it all up, going away, starting over? That's the thing, you can. We all can."

Those summers, at six and seven, all I wanted was to go to Cecil's house, play in the dirt, our bodies at close range. The hours would go by and it felt like we'd become our penises. "Where would you go?" I ask. "Now you're the one sounding ponderous."

"Nepal, Kathmandu. Disappear, Nicholas."

"Which I must do right now, unfortunately. I have to go."

"Certain bars, they should still let you smoke," he says. His voice is generous and wide. "Then I really would feel human. You understand. I know you understand."

3

Back in the office, Nadia pays me no attention. In the U.S. for six years, she hasn't lost her circumflex eyebrows or her miniskirts. On the other hand, as she likes to say, she knows where she is from: a dusty ruins. She holds a stare longer than anyone else I have ever met. She wears a scarf—often in jewel tones—to hold back her chestnut hair from her face, like a peasant or a revolutionary.

On my desk is a binder of information given to me by the developer of the parking lot, Armen Terzian. Armen's father, Arshad, builds mid-grade hotels in in-between spaces along old highways, widened and widened to accommodate traffic, in distant reaches from the city. I read somewhere that Arshad Terzian has built six hotels along the first American highway, Route 30, the "Lincoln Highway." In the same article, published in the *Daily News*, the writer, sitting in the Terzians' sky-blue parlor, in a stone mansion styled like an English country house, respectfully observes the family's prize possession, a full-length portrait of George Washington, presumably by the painter Charles Willson Peale.

Armen Terzian, the son, has a rumpled face, mild except for the Armenian nose, and eyes that appear to wince from a hot wind. As if to compensate, he dresses sharply, with a charcoal suit and purple tie. He takes himself seriously in a touching way, as a dehydrated plant cups its leaves in order to catch any water that it can. Terzian's binder is filled with spreadsheets, thresholds for profit noted in pink highlight. Someone, possibly Terzian himself, has written a description of the apartment house: "not a building, a social center." There are crude renderings, too. The cars on the street are going in the wrong direction.

I can't remember the name of our old bar. It must have changed names three or four times before becoming Kabobeesh. This is almost twenty-five years ago. I don't keep in touch with any of those people. The faces of the bartenders are gone from memory. Only the dim lights and blood-red neon, maybe a brass lamp, a leather banquette, endure. Legs dangle in the dim reaches of my memory.

Nadia leans through the doorway into my private office. Today she's wearing a short-sleeve blue-purple top and a silver ring with a large amethyst stone and chalky eye makeup with a hint of violet. The color coordination is subtler than describing it here, in distant, isolated words, makes it seem. In her earthiness Nadia makes such intention seem natural and easy, a second thought. And so I'm supposed to take note of the color connection—it is after all a flattering color for her desert complexion—and yet forget it, too, as if she herself is an example of effortless design, like a room so contented you forget it has walls. The brown skin of her arms and her neck below the chin is like coffee. Her hair chestnut, her eyes cinnamon, like Eva's. Coffee, chestnut, cinnamon. Back in those days, in our bar, Eva and Reginald and I would laugh at such sorry clichés. We called them cheesy, a favorite word then. The cheesiness lent irony; we could be cheesy, it was in our power. It was in our power to mock others who were actually cheesy. We stood above and beyond. Now the cliché is only that—a sign of laziness, the incapacity to see in specificity, the slow machinations of a near-middle-aged brain. The first time I noticed Nadia, from a distance in a crowded seminar room, I saw Eva, I felt her presence as if she were there. And I couldn't control my gaze. The coffee skin, the chestnut hair, the cinnamon eyes . . . this page from my past bleeds through to the present. Perhaps it has been bleeding all along.

But they aren't equal. No one person is a copy of another. Both Eva and Nadia possess an earthiness and a coolness. For Eva, the coolness is intellectual severity, self-learned and willfully enforced in the West Coast free-love colony where she grew up, and then expected of others around her; for Nadia, it is focus adopted in the desultory chaos of South Beirut. Such focus, calm and self-contained. Half-suspended between our project room and my private office, she awakens me now with the fact of her presence. The light in the room physically lifts, as if struck too by the power of her concentration. The sky, visible through the tall windows across the room, above the southern horizon and the cityscape that looks from this angle rather like a sand drip town, is no longer bleached, or ambivalent.

"You're going?" I say. "It's getting late." Perhaps my mind will clear, free of the pressure, if she leaves, and I'll find a fresh way to approach the Terzian building.

"Tomorrow, you will sign off on the Terzian schedule?" The sound of her voice, like running water, gives me pleasurable pause.

"The work schedule."

"The work schedule you asked me for and I produced last week. Also, the wind and solar analysis is ready."

"Where?"

"On the table out there."

Nadia is determined to build a "net positive" building. Net positive means the building creates more value for the community, for the city, for earth, or humankind, than it takes in energy and resources. Young architects are fond of jargon.

She is right about this, of course. She grasps things quickly; she puts ideas to use.

"You should go. I promise to look at it."

My hands linked behind my head, I stare into the crisp white ceiling. Then I close my eyes and listen for her to walk away. But Nadia is over by the windows when I open my eyes.

"It's so hot the tree is dying," I offer.

"The schedule—tomorrow we'll confirm it? You're avoiding my question—maybe it's the heat. Maybe *you're* dying of heat."

"I may be dying—"

"Not dying, maybe dehydrated. It even bothers me, this humidity."

My desk chair faces the far wall opposite the windows, a deliberate arrangement so that I don't become distracted. A worktable stretches across the room a few feet from the windows. Nadia leans on this table, gazes over at the framed newspaper articles about the 60th Street project and next to them the *Architectural Record* profile of me after I received the AIA award. These things happened before I hired Nadia, but I hadn't bothered to get them framed. She had it done and hung them there one morning last year.

The Terzian building isn't likely to win any awards. Does that concern her? Do I care if we win another award? I'm not sure what it would prove. The work is a reward itself. But as the thought develops, I note a crevice opening inside—a crevice and then a collapse. A forty-five-year-old man caving in slowly, as a tent appears to deflate when one of the structural poles comes free from the grommet. Does Nadia notice the pain in my eyes?

"I bet you didn't really tell anyone about that award . . . Best Young Firm . . ."

"Hardly young . . ."

"Your old colleagues . . . and your ex-wife, I bet you didn't tell her . . . She's an interior designer—"

"Architect. Laura's an interior architect, so of course she knew about it."

Nadia comes over to my desk. "You never told me why you don't have children. Why no children? No family. Just you and her."

"Time went along, I guess."

"Time?"

"Maybe we never had any time. Maybe you can't work sixty, seventy hours a week as we had to and expect to have a family. She didn't really want children until later and then I knew it was too late—not her age but us, it was too late for us. Forget about all that."

"But, tell me the truth, you didn't—you don't—want children? I don't believe you."

"Why?"

"Architects are always thinking of the future . . . No, what I mean: you're sweet, caring. You'd be a great dad. Don't you want a son, a little Nicholas?"

"I dream of little Nicholas," I say, and look back to Nadia. She nods, as if somehow it's in her power, a waitress taking an order. Then she leaves the room.

About ten minutes pass and she returns. She won't let go of something. "Nicholas, tomorrow, then, we'll confirm the schedule? And you said a week ago, we should respond to the request for proposals for an ice cream shop?"

"Gelato."

"Gelato, that's what I meant. Americans are obsessed with gelato. What's the deadline?"

"Maybe the shop should have a case for macarons."

"You really can't combine Italian with French. This is too dangerous."

I begin to get up and think better of it, aware of her gaze that belies the humorous tone of her voice, observing my indifference. And then she slips out.

Below the rim of my glasses the computer screen appears

soft as a cloud. I recall 1989, the year we started going to the bar on 4th Street. I must have spent days that year hunting around. In Indian summer I slid along the old freight tracks that hug the river on the western border of Center City. The air smelled of burnt oil and wild onion and heat. In afternoon I would sweat, especially if a rainstorm was coming. I never minded it. From the river I would walk north to Fairmount, where I live now, or east along South Street. If it rained, I would go inside Book Trader and climb the stairs and look at art anthologies, or giant books of maps from the 1960s, or warped tomes with titles like *Baroque Mexico*, *The Ancients*, *The City as Destiny*. In those days the bookstore was open until midnight. Aimless men, black and white, milled about South Street, making conversation, looking for drugs or sex, or offering. Their voices around corners preceded their faces. They were voices of chalk or plaster, footsteps of eternity.

The voices, the faces, the footsteps: these merge together like a wave of mind and memory. But a real wave that in those days separates me from everyone, as if I don't belong in the neighborhood. In those days, walking these same streets, I would dive in, or under. The turbulence drew me in even as it repelled me. Now, having paced out of my office into our main workspace and under the fluorescent light, the wave breaks at my feet and I scatter, as if afraid for myself. Terzian wants his apartment house—and why not give it to him? What is it that I'm avoiding?

I haven't looked at the project schedule Nadia has drafted, but I begin to leaf through the solar and wind charts, detailed studies that, if we follow them, will tell us how to site the building. Nadia's work is always clear and precise. Yet its impact right now is to make me dull and weary. I switch my mind's eye to Eva, at nineteen, our bodies, our eyes, always in magnetic discourse; we find it nearly impossible to separate ourselves. I think, "If we design for the body . . ." If we did design for the body, even a standard apartment house could have a kind of underlying tactile humanness. A vision comes of a hand touching a surface, a body in space, entering, exiting, moving, and then at rest, people shuffling across space as if on time-lapse, and a building emerging around them, encasing them but also relenting to their touch. Yet how can we design for people first without any attention to form? Structure, mass, and texture, these must wait, as if in hesitant anticipation. The overbearing technical apparatus of my profession must, too.

Most buildings are designed at a distance; in the best case they are composed as form by the god-like hand of the architect, in the worst, by abstract ideas. How foolish this seems in the sudden, explosive moment of consciousness that follows the visceral recollection of Eva's body and mine colliding. The overwhelming vision is of and about myopia: the body up close, claustrophobic, pushes every other consideration away (that's just as it felt at nineteen or twenty . . .). The momentary force of the vision travels from my eyes to my temples and I am sure I feel a kind of tremor as if I'm going to faint. This hasn't ever happened before. I steady myself on the large-format printer.

I recognize that in restoring balance I may lose the impetus; what if it drains away like a vivid dream once exposed to morning consciousness? And so I try to still my focus on the body in place, the human person alive in the world—all architecture must emerge from this embryo. ("Can it be so?" a voice asks and quickly I silence it.) In this way I extend the vision another moment and then another, as a power transforms into possibility. Working past midnight at the wooden table, I create a series of drawings of the "unbuilding," people inhabiting space. I resist the urge to draw quickly as the idea comes, and in time I slow down, tracing imaginary lines of imaginary lives as they move across Terzian's imaginary building.

NATHANIEL POPKIN

Steady and clear of mind, I tell myself that from now on I will trust my instincts and assert my vision. The surging feeling excites me and I nearly gallop back into my office toward the window, but in the darkness I am no longer capable of discerning the view. If I can create architecture to fit a woman or a man . . . Intense myopia settles my vision on this single notion that is, after all, defined by myopia. For the moment I can't see anything else.

4

BACK IN THE OFFICE the next day, Nadia rolls out her drawing paper across the wooden table in the outer office. She has the printer going, too. These are her weapons of action aimed at me. Harvest the olives . . . like a peasant or a revolutionary . . . She is both, opposites perhaps. A peasant is focused on the literal world, the revolutionary on changing it. The peasant persists in the here-and-now and leaves the rest up to a higher power; the revolutionary fixates on the future, twisting the world into a new state. The thought crosses my mind as I gaze at her quietly, and my eyes tear up unexpectedly, in appreciation or intimacy.

Of course we can plot out the schedule. What's needed by August 15: a preliminary rendering, rough, really a feeling; a basic floor plan; some idea of how to handle the flow of people, cars, trash, and noise. "It isn't so simple," she says, the word of God.

Fixated on preserving the vision of last night I speak calmly and slowly. "Let's make this an experiment. We're going to collect the people first, put them in place, design for them. No, let the design come from them."

"I'm supposed to write this in the calendar?"

"Forget the calendar." I say this as if the calendar is the stupidest thing in the world. "Just look." I pull out the pages from the night before: what must appear to her to be a bunch of scribbles.

She doesn't respond, but she looks at me defensively. I ignore it. Her eyes seem to gaze simultaneously in (to confirm the doubt in her mind) and out (to challenge me). I continue on. ". . . Just humans, in place, walking and talking." Does this way of thinking sound ridiculous now? This is the danger.

Her face softens, and I think for a moment of a dentist reaching his arm up above the patient to adjust the yellow light.

"We have the scabby parking lot," I try again. "I want you to put people in it; let them live in it. See—"

The dentist peers in closer . . . "But they need something to live in, in order for us to know anything. There are only thirty days, maybe not even thirty days, not even—"

"Let them go in and out of the ghost building, we don't know how tall or wide, in and out, climb up, turn a knob, carry a bike or a shopping bag, light a cigarette, look out a window, dress for a night out, turn out the lights."

Upstairs, in the office above, it sounds as if a ball is rolling across the floor. When the ball stops, Nadia lets the room go silent. A half a minute passes, perhaps more. "Maybe this is the beginning of a thought," she says, not quite dismissively, with the full flowering of her voice. Nadia's strength of mind recalls Eva's. "But why, Nicholas—why are you asking me to do this? It doesn't make sense."

Why? "Human-centered design." This is a kind of joke between us, meant to lighten the mood.

Ignoring the joke, she says, "I have to refine this schedule and I think you are avoiding it." She pauses. "Maybe you honestly mean these things." Her words are cold; her voice compassionate, humane. I might have said, "I want an architecture that matches the tone and texture of your voice." Instead, I fixate on the words, now invasive, like a draft that seeps through the floorboards, and I dare not press any advantage I feel I have. Last night's overpowering vision is beginning to weaken—and the words I try to use are without tangible meaning.

Nadia says, voice and words edging closer now, "I'm not going to bother you with this right now."

She turns her head, like a seasoned swimmer snatching breath, with calm intent, and plunges it back into work. She recognizes my crisis of faith because she sees right through me. The wail of confidence from last evening already seems dry and distant. Doubt presses in instead and unanswerable questions follow, as ambivalence collects after masturbation.

Nadia draws by hand because she was trained in Beirut and Tunis and can't imagine working only in CAD. The day we met, at a symposium on carbon-neutral construction, she said she didn't understand why young American architects aren't taught to draw. "Everyone talks about human-centered design, but they forget about the human hand!"

Her idealism was striking. "But you liked studying architecture here?"

"I like everything about this country."

And then, as if to deflect the presence of Eva, of this person who might be Eva, I said, "You should be honest."

"I mean it." Nadia's stare grounds any dissent. Far less intellectual in her thinking than Eva, she conveys certainty based in some primordial fact.

What do I want to say now, in our office? That I trust her to make me see what I can't? Can I admit that, far differently from her, I feel that I am out of answers, that I doubt even the merit of the architectural award? Isn't innovation itself a kind of formula or at least owing to someone else's concept? The breaking of a mold only later becomes a new mold . . . Can I admit that even with Nadia I've lost the strength of vision needed to guide a man like Terzian, that I'm seized by the fear that architecture has been kidnapped by abstract ideas? Not merely profit thresholds. Sustainability, materials, system efficiencies, form . . .

Finally I respond. "Everything we do as architects is based on ideas, notions, tastes, prevailing best practices someone else has figured out that are the same all across the world."

"You say this as if it's a problem," she says. She stares and I stare back, only so long. "Please tell me, does originality really exist? I want to hear."

All I can do is shrug. How do I say that I feel like a fraud? I form the words in my mind and yet I say nothing. Instead, for a moment I recall Eva, in the flush of love, wanting me to face questions bravely. Love, she says, makes her patient with me, more patient than she's ever been in her life. Our own love, for example, won't work if we are to imagine it is the answer to a need. "But what if we say it is a never-ending question, and live with that?" she asserts. "No finality, no trap."

After a long pause, I say to Nadia, "How is it possible that a design can be right for this specific moment in time, in this specific place, in this street, which isn't the same, can't be the same as any other place?"

Sensing a way to advance the task at hand and to end the conversation, Nadia calls up the address on Google Maps. She clicks to Street View. The clouds are low across the sky, but they cast no shadow over the lot. It's midday, summer. It says June at the top of the page. Weeds are only starting to reach through the posts in the black metal fence, aluminum meant to look like it might be wrought iron. Black letter graffiti on the sidewalk mirrors black letter graffiti on the east wall of an old commercial building at the front of the lot. And there, in the foreground, walking east, head down, is Popkin, the poet. It looks like he's carrying a magazine. He carries it folded up under his arm like an incidental musket. Nadia slides the date bar to the right. Popkin vanishes. Now a gray-haired man walks his dog one step behind where Popkin had been. The graffiti is gone. Identical clouds stretch low across the skyline. Later I will realize the gray-haired man is Joe Russakoff, son of the legendary bookseller Jerome Russakoff. His own store, a block away, is called Mostly Books. Back one point on the timeline, Russakoff disappears. The sidewalk is empty. A man loads a sports car's hubcap into his open sedan, standard issue. Graffiti reappears, evaporates, and clouds tumble across the top of the frame.

The poet Popkin is a sly devil. He leaves poems on park benches, café tables, under trees. "Each poem is for someone, I just don't know who," he tells me. We are having beer at our old bar, where Kabobeesh is now. It is one of the last times I go there, the long year after everyone else has left. We discuss the religious instinct in poetry. I ask, stupidly, if he is a religious poet. "All poetry is religious," he says.

Then he says, "It's the religion of almost."

5

NADIA SAYS, "I don't go to South Street, so I can't tell you what it's like 'these days.'" She mimics my old-fashioned turn of phrase. South Street is behind the parking lot where the apartment building will go. Once, until 1854, it was the southern border of the city. "The shopkeepers are either Arab or Israeli." And so? "And so I just can't deal with it." I don't know who the shopkeepers are. I had thought they were still hippies.

A highway, the Crosstown Expressway, would have obliterated South Street and the neighborhoods on either side, those that were originally in the city and those that until 1854 were across the lawless border. When it seemed like the highway plan was going to be pushed through, the hippies and the housing activists and the old Polish ladies organized. The architect Denise Scott Brown led the protests, I tell Nadia. She must be very old now. She is a woman of moral clarity. This was the 1960s into the 70s. The Jewish department store owners sold out before they lost everything. *Mikey and Nicky* takes place then, after they have vanished.

What else has vanished? Who lived around South Street one hundred years ago, or one hundred fifty? A map from 1895, which I find easily on the Internet, shows a street cutting through where the parking lot is now. Just as I had thought. But I am wrong about the orientation of the street. I have misread the ruins. Instead of east to west, the little street runs south to north from Bainbridge to South. It's called Charles Street. Another, a tiny alley, called McLaughlin's Court, is trapped in the middle, accessible only through the South Street Distillery on the north. A market takes up the center of Bainbridge Street for two blocks in front of the parking lot. This is why the street here is twice as wide as a normal street. Across from the market is a synagogue, and next to it, a dispensary. There is a second synagogue on 5th Street, and below that, on a triangular lot, Snellenburg's Department Store, another distillery, a soap factory, a meeting hall. Drawn by hand and shaded pink, the map shows the South Street Distillery's three circular vats, a curious detail the mapmaker included.

The graffiti on our old bar goes down the alley from 4th Street toward 3rd. In 1895 this alley is called Trout. Other blocks of the same alley, as it continues east and west, are called Alaska, Emeline, and Bradford. By 1910, as I learn, overlaying an atlas from that year on the one from 1895, the names Trout, Alaska, Emeline, and Bradford have disappeared. All the alleys are called Kater. The market has been removed. In a semicircle around the block of the parking lot there are now five synagogues. One of them is labeled "Jewish church."

On the computer screen, multiple pasts soak into the present like clouds of various chemical compounds infusing a clear solution. If Nadia demands to know what I am doing, I could say I'm conducting experiments.

Toggling back and forth between maps, 1895 to 1910, 1910 to 1895: a large building, "Young Women's Union," replaces three or four smaller ones. I've seen a photograph of this building, which no longer exists. It has the look of a collegiate hall. Time passes, and on the map a man's hand marks the change in precise detail using the latest science. And yet it is his hand. He writes "Colored Bethel Church." He writes "St. Stanislaus R.C. Church." But he doesn't name the synagogues. What does he think about the Jewish and Catholic immigrants? Do they make him feel uneasy? Or is he one, too?

What will my apartment building have to say to all of this? Nadia would suggest, cunningly, that it should speak. But one day it too will be gone.

Scrolling the streets of 1910 is a game of discovery. You can move quickly from one street to the next, one neighborhood to the next. As the map moves, the present-day map peeks through and then the 1895 map spills over it, like paint, and then another coat, the atlas of 1910. Train tracks like the raised veins of a leaf bifurcate Washington Avenue and curl to connect to the factories and coal yards on either side. Time overlaps on this street in the present day, with its remnants of iron works alongside Vietnamese *phở* houses and Buddhist temples. I wonder if we can compose a building for Terzian that overlaps, gesturing to its neighbors, touching the past without erasing it. But some in my profession deny this is architecture. They believe only in originality. As I note this, wishing to believe in honesty, in the trail of ideas from one generation to the next, in architecture as conversation, doubt creeps in and fear again of my own weakness and fraudulence, swift and ugly, blots out everything else.

At the wooden table in the outer office, Nadia eats lunch, noodles from a takeout container. She works while she eats. She has gone ahead and transferred her project schedule to a white sheet large enough to hang on the wall. I admire her resilience. Around her, she has stacked files, plans, and papers related to the commission. One of them is the developer's profit threshold spreadsheet, unfolded next to an environmental report on the parking lot done by an engineering firm. I've never seen the environmental analysis. She marks it up with yellow highlighter. When she was a child, in 1996, a stray Israeli bomb landed fifty feet from Nadia and her mother leaving a bakery (she will never be able to eat *za'atar* again). The bomb destroyed the small gymnasium where she had learned to climb ropes. Nadia's practical impulse, her attraction to ideas extracted from facts, was born on that day, and she followed it to the United States.

One day in January, as wet snow blotted the window in my office, I pulled an old bottle of Veuve Clicquot out of the refrigerator and I put two glasses on the table, just where Nadia is sitting now. That morning we had submitted a proposal for a new building at a small private school and felt we had reason to celebrate (particularly proud of our flexible classrooms). A trustee of the school was a client of my old firm; this was reason enough to feel confident.

"Do you know why I came to work for you?" she asked, after a second glass of champagne.

"The expensive booze."

"Yes, actually, I noticed that . . . OK, maybe that's it."

"The luxury office . . ."

She stared warmly, with a slight look of audacity I didn't notice at first. I filled the glasses a third time. "Maybe you can guess again." The cinnamon eyes . . .

"No, I stand on principle—luxury booze and fancy offices."

"Then I guess I won't tell you. I'll put the bottle away." She pronounced "bottle" with a distinctly Lebanese accent, doubling the L. "Two reasons, really."

"Baultal," I hear . . .

"You really don't want to know?"

I folded my arms. She sipped her champagne, the liquid gold illuminating her face.

"Do you not know already? It's obvious. You said, that first time we met and you asked if I was looking for a job—you made me feel immediately equal. Not that I believed you or that you believed it. But you made me feel this way."

"Clearly I was—"

"Maybe you didn't realize, Mr. Moscowitz."

"You don't miss much."

"You want to know the second reason? It is a better reason."

"OK. But wait. The champagne is almost gone." I poured the rest.

"I only trust tall men."

We might have moved just then to the Happy Rooster, or I might have taken her to my house and made her one of my father's best recipes. She was willing to seduce me right there in the office, below the snow-muted window or on the wooden table . . . But I turned off my computer, put the bottle in the recycling bucket, and told Nadia I would drive her home (I had the car that day in order to deliver our proposal for the private school building). She bolted from the car after a kiss on both cheeks, calmly masking her disappointment or humiliation, and I drove up along the Delaware River with the snow now slowed and quiet and swirling, as if the river were a wall. I imagined the car bouncing off the wall.

Nadia finishes her noodles and looks up at me. "A building can't have a soul until it is inhabited," she says (she has never spoken of that night and I pretend it never happened), rolling out her drawing paper. "People give it soul. So you are right." Her voice is tight and unforgiving. She gestures with her elbow on the table, palm up. Her arms make her seem like she isn't a compact human (she is), but her arms are deceiving. They are an athlete's arms, I think unconsciously, and later I recognize that it is Eva I am seeing at the wooden table, not Nadia.

Had I moved closer to Nadia the night we shared the bottle of Veuve Clicquot . . . had she seduced me at the wooden table and had I complied . . . had I pulled down the wall dividing the personal and the professional . . . But the wall is a guard against cruelty, against the possibility of self-betrayal. A sweet sadness for her comes over me. She must sense my gaze. Nadia rejects pity, particularly if it's aimed at her.

And so she goes on, "After the first inhabitants give the building its soul, then others come and the soul of the building adapts," now with her eyes fixed to mine. I half-smile at her bravery. "The original soul goes through a period of negotiation, an unsettling period, until it finally settles."

"But it doesn't ever settle." I must reengage, and yet the heat has made me tired.

"Maybe it does and maybe it doesn't," she answers, proving herself the fiercer and the wiser.

The worktable: it is identical to the table in the dining room of the house on 49th Street, where I recall Eva slicing through Kant and Hegel and then Kierkegaard. My mother had shipped two tables from Holland when her family's bakery closed; for years my father used them in his restaurants. When times were good, we ate as a family at the back of the restaurant, at this table, with the knife scars of three generations. The other table, the one that arrived for me in a yellow van on a drizzly August day with leather brown leaves sailing to the brick sidewalk, is lost. I must have left it there, on 49th Street, during the darkness of that spring many years ago.

Have I brought Nadia into my firm (into my life) because she recalls Eva?

Like Eva, she possesses no apparent determination; she has the kind of will that doesn't need it. Is it that will I wish to share, to push me forward? It seems cruel of me to expect it. She's my employee; I pay her salary. She owes me nothing more.

6

I TELL NADIA I'm going to meet a prospective client for coffee. He's renovating an old machine shop, I say, and invent a story about fire damage and a collapsed wall. I add, for the sake of veracity, "Maybe we don't want to touch it."

"And the ice cream proposal?"

"The what?"

"Sorry, gelato. Gelato and macarons."

"No—it won't work. Didn't I tell you? I decided . . . didn't make sense for the office."

I order a small cup of vanilla yogurt at the Yogorino and carry it to Rittenhouse Square. But I don't sit long enough to finish it. I try to listen for the birds beneath the din of the square and the trucks and taxis going by on Walnut Street as one listens for a particular instrument in the orchestra, but I can't hear them. Perhaps the heat has sapped their strength. I get up to leave. The sun is nearly straight up—there is no shade, even along the walls of the buildings. I move apprehensively across Walnut and then across Sansom, and Chestnut, where a frame shop keeps a giant gilt-framed mirror on the sidewalk to entice the passerby. I envision flames.

A few minutes later, I arrive at Logan Square, which is really a traffic circle inside a square that's also cut off by an underground expressway that's unfortunately mostly open to the sky, like an incision in the city. And yet inside the circle that's inside the half-sliced square is a magical fountain named for a man named Swann (the name itself lends a kind of fairy-tale air), where water leaps from the mouths of catfish, turtles, frogs, and, of course, swans.

The sun here draws and repels. Children, some prepared in bathing suits, others in shorts and T-shirts, play in the fountain, jumping over the sculptural frogs and turtles. The water sprays between their legs. Every child is soaked, water clinging shirt to skin with magnet force, onyx hair in layers, like models of continental plates, pushed from forehead and mounded on top as if formed from sculptural clay.

In summer as a boy, too old to run naked around Cecil Baxter's lawn, I accompanied my father, Lawrence Alan Moscowitz, called Larry, to the market and sometimes to the couple of farms that supplied his restaurant directly. I recall one particular farmer, a man in his sixties, perhaps, wiry, red-faced, and oblivious to me, even as I climbed on the equipment and threw rocks into his field. My father never instructed me yes or no. Sometimes I found myself in the farmhouse standing on an uneven floor, the farmer's wife in her stained housedress and blotchy skin ordering me to sit down at the rose-colored Formica table and placing a piece of cake and a glass of milk in front of me. She stared at me down her long nose—"sharp as a bird's beak," my father and I laughed later, the truck pitching machine gun–like down the dirt road— as if to overturn her husband's utter indifference or disinterest or blindness, whatever it was, her eyes burning into my head from behind, measuring my moral fitness according to how quickly and how much milk I drank. "You're a regular *schvartze*," she would say, "as dark as the ones they show playing baseball on TV." In summer, it was true, as a kid I turned a dark olive, so that my hair and skin quite nearly matched. I understood the farmer's wife, but I didn't, really. My father had neglected to expose me much to baseball or to his Bronx relatives who might be known to toss around *schvartze* in derisive tone, though the word left the woman's mouth as a mangled remainder of Pennsylvania Dutch and not, certainly, a whisper of Yiddish.

I sit at the edge of the fountain; the wind sprays the water intermittently on my back. A text from Cecil: he thinks I need a break, some time at the beach. "Come to my mother's East Hampton house? She'd love to see you. Escape the heat!" Cecil is right. It's too hot to stay long sitting by the fountain. I type out: "I wish!" Then I delete, letter by letter. I write instead, "Let me think about it." I delete that, then write, "Too much work." I hit send.

"You're ungrateful," appears seconds later. Then: "Really, I insist. What could be so important?"

The main city library faces Logan Square on the north side. Inside the neoclassical library, which is a copy of the Comte de Crillon's palace that faces the Place de la Concorde: the air of a tomb. At nineteen, I came here the first time in search of William Klein's *New York*. Someone at school had said, as if repeating a permanent fact, that the Parkway, the diagonal boulevard that runs through Logan Square from City Hall to the Museum of Art, was the "Champs-Élysées of Philadelphia." This may have been an ad man's copy (and thus untrue) that became a joke. The Parkway, like much of the city in the 1980s, felt jagged and broken, and Styrofoam cups collected in the weeds. The "Champs-Élysées of Philadelphia" was aspiration or derision, or both, but also the first indication, to me, that one city might borrow from another.

In the tomb air, the Indian summer day I came here in search of Klein's *New York* drifts into the present like a dissipating cloud. I need the book for a paper on "street photography and the concept of movement." Klein moves and the people move and the city moves, like three overlapping planes of existence. It is a loose thesis, but born of love for the concept of the city and for Eva, who loves me, she says, because I believe in myself. I discover that the gray tone of the plaster, the worn marble of the floor, the high, soft light of the library calm me so that I can think and observe, and from that day I start coming here. The campus library does me no good. It makes me tense, or I will sleep for hours at a time, sometimes sweating in the aluminum light of the autumn sun intensified by the window next to my carrel, enduring rabid dreams. Finally awake, what is this? The feeling of shame.

August 15. The date floats in my mind. This is our deadline to produce a plan, in concept, with rough floor plans and renderings for Armen Terzian to present to the neighbors. Nadia has made a schedule because I haven't. Like Eva, she responds to a challenge by grasping for what's real. Perhaps she wishes to save me from myself. Here, on the second floor of the library, in the social sciences room, will the librarian show me books that might help me understand the neighborhood around the parking lot where I am to build the apartment house? "Do you have a library card, do you know how to use the catalog?" she responds with an edge to her voice. I stutter in my response before searching out the woman's warm gray eyes. It is the same librarian whom I had asked for the William Klein, the same librarian scornful of the young love I must have so obviously betrayed, though she herself couldn't have been much older. That day, my first time in this long room, she points over my shoulder. I must cross the hall, to art.

The librarian has aged well; her hair is silver and her cheeks shine; she hasn't been dulled by decades sitting in this same seat behind this same desk in this same room. In fact, the opposite. She is radiant. And now I see: the indifference is a manner of self-protection; the indifference is subversion. I walk away.

I do as she says and enter keywords into the catalog. All the books I need are in one section, and I begin pulling titles, unsure even of what I'm grabbing. An architect ought to be analyzing the path of the sun as it moves across the parking lot, measuring the wind, setting up the excavator to take core samples. Perhaps modeling mass and volume, reading and re-reading the building code. Though Nadia has probably done these things already.

But what if an architect is searching for something else?

Now I have one of those books of historical photographs that exist for every town and neighborhood in America. Sepia-toned, the historical record. This one is for South Street. Here is a picture looking east from 5th Street, around the corner from Terzian's parking lot. Here is Dubrow's furniture store, shot up one day in the 1970s by members of the Black Mafia. Here is Sam Ponnock inside his comic book and toy "empire," Valentine's Day, 1931. Here is Levis Hot Dogs twenty years later, a police officer leaning on the takeout window. He wears his collar open and his tie down, like a foreman who's just gotten rid of some troublemakers off the factory floor. He must be waiting for his freebie, a hot dog with two fish cakes, a dose of sauerkraut. Levis, says the photo citation, was sent by his parents to Philadelphia from Lithuania to escape the Czar's army.

Does any of this leave a stamp?

The librarian is behind me. How long has she been standing there? I turn around, but now she is by the bookshelf and she brings me a title, *The Jewish Quarter of Philadelphia*. She presses the cover with her finger as she places the book before me. Her fingers are long and elegant and her nails are mani-cured and painted midnight blue. I accept the book as a gesture of reconciliation, but she pulls away quickly and collides with a nearby table. "I'm sorry," I say, "for all the trouble." She doesn't respond. Only now her clapping heels disturb the room.

At the back of the book is a page from the 1910 atlas, in black and white. The Crystal Palace Theatre is just north of the parking lot site, but I'd missed it when I was looking at the atlas on the computer. Of course, this is the Theater of the Living Arts, where some nights, all those years ago, we might go to our bar early and then attend the midnight showing of the *Rocky Horror Picture Show*. Reginald goes as Magenta but I never dress for the show. *Rocky Horror* has been going on for a decade at least at the T.L.A., and we, all of us who live in the house at 417 S. 49th Street, know it and feel, even as we swell with originality, that we are trying to capture something that isn't rightly ours. Yet all we are doing is following tradition, or beginning it. We must tell ourselves it's the second generation that turns an impulse into a cultural form.

The Crystal Palace is the first nickelodeon in the neighborhood. Soon after: the Princess, the Hippodrome, and the Model. Above the description of the Princess in the book is a block quote. It begins, "Anarchism and Atheism were very popular among the young immigrants." This is according to Charles Cohen, who at thirteen works at a newsstand at 5th and South, the first stand to sell Yiddish papers. Cohen dabbles in atheism, he says. "It relieved one of doing the things that a believer is supposed to do."

The year I turn thirteen, my mother moves in with a painter named Edmund. My father decides I must have a bar mitzvah; his insistence is irrational, and uncharacteristic of a man without taste for religion or parental coercion, but looking back I realize he is building a wall against my mother's betrayal. He leaves the restaurant midday to pick me up and drive me to lessons with a rabbi and cantor from a Reform temple that allows the children of Jewish fathers and non-Jewish mothers to consider themselves Jewish. Luckily for my father, by car, the synagogue is only twenty minutes from my school. The problem is that he has to rush immediately back to the restaurant and so somehow arranges for the cantor, a humorless figure in brown polyester pants and a worn tweed coat, to drive me home when the lesson is over. I sit uncomfortably in his overheated car breathing in the brine of the imitation leather seats, resenting my ridiculous, arbitrary father with his wild beard—"the crumb nest," my mother calls it—his figure of Sisyphus, never abetting in his hope for culinary perfection. "You'll forgive him one day," says the cantor. At the time, sweating in the back seat (a mess of crumpled files, old newspapers, sandwich wrappers, and a dusty black transistor radio occupies the front passenger seat), the cantor's willful perceptiveness presses in on me like a hand over the mouth and I feel as though I can't breathe. How can I go along with this? There is no way I can do it and yet I do, with the clairvoyant cantor nudging me to memorize the Hebrew sounds. What do they mean, these sounds? "That the glowing light of God travels with us, wherever we are," the rabbi suggests, and I nod, repressing a yawn. Along with the rabbi, I read the English translation, "the sum of the things for the tabernacle." I want to ask if the dimensions of the tent, the materials, the colors of the fabric, the stones used for the breastplate over the Torah, if these things matter. If not, what am I doing memorizing the words?

God is merciful, and the bar mitzvah finally comes. We have the luncheon at the restaurant; my mother, Hilda, shows up late, with rings of turquoise or sapphire or both, I can't recall. She turns to me in a half gaze and I try to ignore her. I let her touch my hair, as if she is gesturing at a shadow. My father busies himself with the food. The lamb must be perfect, a detail I can't fathom. It is light now until six and this surprises me; when I duck out the kitchen door of the cramped restaurant and stare across the street, the sun's distant light is filtering through the slender gray trunks of the trees. For some reason the Hebrew chanting enraptures my mind, but I have the sensation, already, of misplacing it. And then it disappears.

Here is a photograph of the Washington Market, which opens in 1857 in front of Armen Terzian's parking lot site and extends from 3rd to 5th Streets. It is a butcher's market originally; each peddler sells one kind of meat: goat, lamb, pork, or beef. The author of *The Jewish Quarter*, Harry Boonin, writes in his description of the market that one mutton butcher sells the meat of five hundred sheep in one week. When the market closes in 1903, it leaves a permanent stamp, like a thumbprint. Bainbridge Street remains today more than twice as wide as a normal street, and shaded by oak and maple trees that run along the center of it, a hesitant half gesture to the Parisian boulevard. Yet the shade is real.

Where is the librarian? I stand up but don't see her. I want to tell her the book is just right. The book is leading me somewhere. My chair against the polished floor lets out a trumpet note, slashing the silence of the reading room as if answering the gash sound of her heels. But the librarian's chair is empty.

For some reason I drift out of the long room and into the hallway and then into the art department. The photography books are on the left. Nothing seems to have changed, as if they haven't added any new titles. Perhaps photographers don't publish books anymore. I recall the greedy mouths, delirious, manic faces of the people in William Klein's book, the myopia of his lens. I pull out the card in the pocket attached to the inside back cover. The last time someone has borrowed this book: OCT 2009. I scan the dates from the present to the first, JAN 1986. It must have been September or October 1989 when I brought this book to 417 S. 49th Street and set it on the wooden table my father had abandoned and that I would, too, later, but I don't see that date. DEC 1989 is stamped in blue, but that would have been too late. Have I printed this event in memory in error? Confused the date, or confused the book? How can I experience something and then substitute details, as if all memory is rewriting?

Back in the social sciences department I am careful to preserve the hush. A different librarian sits in the chair now, a man about thirty-eight with greasy hair. Boonin's book, like a half-eaten pear, is still open to a photograph of the Washington Market. I flip back and then forward a page or two. After a moment, I trip on "Moskovitz." Moskovitz almost exactly like me. But not only Moskovitz, Moskovitz of Bainbridge Street, the same part of the street, in the same neighborhood, as Terzian's parking lot: "Moskovitz, an anarchist, had a stand opposite the synagogue at 322 Bainbridge Street."

7

WHO IS THIS Louis Moskovitz? An immigrant, I suppose, caught up in "anti-religious fervor." Boonin, the historian, says that Moskovitz opens his stand on Yom Kippur morning, 1889. He is a grain seller. Across the street from his stand is a synagogue belonging to Chevra Ahavath Chesed, the Brotherhood of Love of Mercy. The name of the synagogue also identifies the founders and where they are from: Anshe Shavel, the Men of Shavel. Shavel is a town in Lithuania, I discover, in the north. The Internet, which I access in the library, tells me it is written like this in Lithuanian: Šiauliai. Lithuania looks like a squat, miniature Africa. Šiauliai matches up, approximately, to Sabhā, a small city in the Libyan desert. سبها is how it is written in Arabic (online, one thing leads to another). It is shaped like a boulder, with a ring road enclosing it like the shell of an egg. Shavel, Šiauliai, is like an X, or a four-legged spider. The spider, with its long legs, taps the shell of the egg, it wraps it in silk, it weaves a cloud to protect the egg city from the incessant heat. The Lithuanians crawl across the ocean to come to Bainbridge Street. But how can the neighborhood feel anything like Shavel? Do the men build Love of Mercy to fulfill a memory? There is a photograph of the building next to the story about Moskovitz. The photograph is from 1943. The synagogue, with its Hebrew writing still intact on the awning over the door, has nearly burned down. Half the windows are gone, the façade, licked by flame, is blackened. A boy and a girl, he in shorts and a collar shirt and she in a dress, survey the damage. Do they know what is happening to their cousins in Lithuania, in France, in Poland, in Germany?

Places have an intrinsic relation: even after the fire, the building in Philadelphia says "Shavel," one city imprinting itself on another. And yet the ink is thin. What do these places really have to do with each other? As little, perhaps, as the palace of the Comte de Crillon on the Place de la Concorde has to do with the main branch of the Free Library on Logan Square. No: the Shavel synagogue is more than an aspirational gesture; it is an act of faith. But what might it have to do with the Bainbridge Street of today? Or with Terzian's apartment house?

"What are you doing?" reads Nadia's text. I click it off. What am I doing? I put the phone down, pick it up, put it down, pick it up, and write out, "thinking about the project." I possess terrifying, arbitrary power. This frightens me. Either we do it and get paid . . . or? I walk away—let her loose, let myself loose. I start to think Cecil is right.

Nadia always draws in pencil, on a long white sheet. She prefers rolls of drawing paper that remind her of undergraduate days in Beirut. She draws with precision, as if to say nothing for her is conceptual. Only certain male architects seem to make heroic pencil sketches to assert artistic genius. I imagine her now, in the office, while I wade through books, searching . . . her hair gathered in a low, loose bun. A glancing hand will unwind it.

Moskovitz decides to provoke the members of Love of Mercy by opening his stand in the Washington Market on Yom Kippur, the holiest day of the year, writes the historian Boonin. Doing business on that day is strictly forbidden. Moskovitz has planned this attack. Like a chemical weapon, it will strike the nerve. It will cause a palsy. Facing Love of Mercy, he stands erect with wide shoulders and dresses himself for prayer, in white robe and fringed shawl, the clothing that itself is integral to prayer. And he recites his lines, not from Torah, not from the book of prayer, with its precise rabbinic arrangement fought over and refined through the centuries, but from the anarchist doctrine of Johann Most or the Yiddish anarchist paper *Fraye Arbeter Shtime*. Moskovitz releases his gas.

How old is this Moskovitz? Boonin doesn't say. But as I read on, a picture emerges of a man about twenty-two, who having grown up in a religious family in a poor, peasant village in the Pale of Settlement, perhaps even in Lithuania, rejects the assumption of God. What kind of merciful God allows misery and injustice, the death of small children, their mothers in birth, their fathers abused and then sent off to war? God, if he exists, thinks Moskovitz, is a God to be feared. And fear provokes aggression.

Is Moskovitz delirious with fear? Or do his eyes glint with devilish self-assurance? With his subversive plan, he is laying a trap.

When I am about that age, or younger—yes, younger by a year—we feel it necessary to organize to protect the environment. Wetlands are disappearing, the ozone layer is about shot, toxic chemicals and fertilizers are turning our rivers into cesspools. I justify the impulse: we must put bodies in the way of polluters. We must sacrifice ourselves for the good of the earth. The twentieth anniversary of Earth Day is coming up—it's up to us to continue the movement. It must be the winter or spring after I write the paper on movement in the photography of William Klein. Afraid of exposing herself, Eva has begun pushing me away. She cloaks the fear in reason. I am seeking answers, she says, instead of asking questions, and that is why I want to protest a plan to expand the refineries along the river. Protest is a definitive answer. "It fills you with venom, like a rabid dog," she says. "Rabies is an ingenious virus," says Reginald, who is sitting with us at the wooden bakery table inside the house on 49th Street. Reginald lives there with us and two other roommates, Harris, a mathematician, and Abigail, who studies folklore. Popkin is in love with Abigail, but he doesn't live in the house, which is far from other student apartments. The distance makes us feel haughty and proud. Reginald's room is in the third-floor attic, under the pitched roof. The house front is stucco framed by a lattice of Tudor trim and below that stone and English windows. An identical house joins ours on the south. "Rabies turns its vector, almost always dogs, into an army of proliferation," Reginald says. His major is called "Biological Basis of Behavior."

"Industrial pollution is a kind of rabies, then," I think but don't say, wary for some reason of inciting Eva.

Reginald is being clever for Eva's sake; he sides with her. Perhaps it is mutual. Perhaps she is trying to get to him through me.

Eva has survived growing up in a free-love commune, near Seattle. She doesn't use the word "survived"; it is too dramatic and final. "People change . . ."

"They make choices," I say, prodding.

"If by choice, you mean decide on an answer, no, that's not it."

We have this argument repeatedly. She wants something from me that I don't know how to give. When I give too much she pushes away. The repeated abstract argument is a wall to protect her heart.

"You have to open up," she says, turning her own fear around, deflecting. By now, in the argument, she is laughing. She forgives easily but argues relentlessly (she has decided to go on to study law). Her forgiveness is an oasis that seems infinitely deep; it drives my twenty-year-old self wild. The savagery of our intimacy might last for days and then end with a proposal, something like: "Let's take the Kierkegaard seminar." I barely know who Kierkegaard is. "The philosopher of intentional confusion," she answers, and her eyes reach for mine. Eagerly I acquiesce.

To reward me for agreeing to take the seminar with her she agrees to accompany me on the first march against the refineries. We hold hands walking down Spruce Street into the glare of television cameras. The house is empty when we get home that night. Ice has formed on the step and Eva slips. She clutches herself oddly, as if she's pulled a hamstring. We are sitting inside the English windows holding each other against the draft when she says, "I had an abortion. I just want you to know."

Louis Moskovitz, in his shawl and in his robe, dovens an anti-prayer on Yom Kippur, 1889. That's how I see it, the open text lying back like spread legs on the wooden library table, in the stardust air. The shadow of the bull-like man rocks in the clarifying autumn light, words emitting like a startling wind. Inside the synagogue, with the temperature rising, a group of men (certainly), even thicker and heavier than Moskovitz as I imagine him, pushes through the door and into the north-facing shadow. It is cool, God has struck the humidity, but now the thick maduro air, in the shade at least, is becoming brittle. What a sensation, spring's opposite is also a gift of life. Two of them catch a look at Moskovitz. The gas hits. They forget the whisper prayers, the meaning of them not the sound, which now intensifies, Moskovitz's and theirs, Moskovitz's and theirs, as they come closer, back into light, first the two and then others. The space between the men and Moskovitz shortens. He doesn't move except his lips. The bull gives no ground. Their limbs, because of the gas, shake and welter. Spittle emits, in self-betrayal, from their Shavel tongues.

One of the men grabs hold of Moskovitz's book of Most. Another claws at the sacred fringe of the shawl and between his own fringe and Moskovitz's fringe the threads intermix like high school mouths, like first-time deviants. The violation of the sacred day is like filament shuddering alive. Now there is gas and there is current. No prayerful man is safe from himself. The men, now six or eight of them, completely erase the distance between themselves and Moskovitz. Head coverings fall to the dusty ground. The Most drops too. A foot drags across the back of Moskovitz's knees and, whispering still, the anarchist catches himself. Does he call out, "For the love of mercy?" It doesn't say. But the look of the whole exchange as witnessed by a policeman on the corner, either at 3rd or 4th Street, elicits an instant response. The religious are thrown in a paddy wagon and swept away for disturbing the peace.

As a young man, food takes hold of my Bronx-raised father and turns his nose, his touch, his eyes into living spirits. This happens in France, in Cassis, at a restaurant called Six Chats. There are probably restaurants all over the south of France with this name, for some reason, but here, in a back alley, uphill from the sea two and a half blocks, he tastes bouillabaisse and then my mother, who lives upstairs. She is Dutch, and insists I be called Nicholas, like a king.

Six Chats lives inside him, even after they have left France and moved to River Road. He keeps that place in mind as he works in the kitchen of his first restaurant, so that every dish can contain the essence of it, the market, the cliffs, the salt, the bouillabaisse, the act of falling in love. In those days his eyes glisten. By the time my mother leaves, his beard has already begun to gray. At sixteen, three years after the bar mitzvah, I begin to appreciate the vital contradiction of his nature: a sloppy man, he is an idealist, a perfectionist. The contradiction works itself out in failure. As other men drink to excess or cheat on their wives, my father fails. Once he cautions me, "Don't be like me." The rest of the time he barely seems to notice whether I'm aware of his melancholy.

The library is full of whisperers, but one, a dark-skinned man with plump fingers shiny as kidneys, with a pile of books before him, has been whispering since I arrived in the reading room. It isn't clear if he is reading aloud.

Moskovitz. Boonin calls him "the apostate," but with cheek, to set up a narrative turn. One day, he will walk away from the radical life to become the leader of the Jewish burial society. "Its membership included the most devout and God-fearing in the community."

8

IT'S ALREADY SEVEN in the evening when I emerge from the library. Most of the sky has turned solid black, glossy as ink drying, and it smells electric. The lowering sun in the west is like a spotlight on the fountain in the foreground. The fountain is solid white. Here is the world as if recorded on a negative. For several minutes I can't look away. It is as if the world I inhabit, on the steps of the library, and the world beyond are distinct; I've left one to enter the other. But where is the door? And what will happen if I walk south toward the office and then further into the inked darkness, toward the parking lot? I have a feeling I will disappear.

My house, on Aspen Street, is ten minutes from the library. I walk gingerly west and then north. The sky in this direction is like an old bruise—purple, green, and gold. Occasionally I turn around to gaze at the other world, the one in negative. About eight minutes into the walk, the foreground behind me dissolves to gray, and when I turn back around to face north everything everywhere is black, and the worlds combine. Even the rain that has begun, like black ink, blots out the light.

Around nine that night, Cecil calls. He's going to leave for East Hampton tomorrow after work. "I'll drive and you can sleep if you want. You seem tired."

"I appreciate the concern."

"No, really."

"Can I call you tomorrow?"

"You're still ungrateful, Moscowitz. Something's up. And it's not your wife since you're not married anymore. So it's a girlfriend or it's your work. Or something in the far reaches of that dense head of yours."

"I wish I knew."

"My mother will cook for us."

"Give me a few weeks. You'll go out there again?"

"I will."

"Then August."

"Then August."

The next day, Friday, the rain continues intermittently. I go for coffee and recognize I am gone a long time; when I leave the café it's raining again and I get soaked walking back. My feet step gingerly on the slippery white painted wooden floor of the main work studio. Nadia ignores me. Moskovitz in front of Love of Mercy wishes to tear down the tabernacle. Is that what I desire too?

Ten minutes after I come in, when I don't emerge from my private office, Nadia appears in the doorway. "Maybe you don't see it, but Terzian is laying you a trap," she says, annunciating slowly. "Even though he seems to care about the quality of his building, he's really mostly interested in your name."

For a moment I hear only the sound of her voice, the stream of it, and not the words. "Mr. Moscowitz!" This is another joke between us, and I look up. "I know this," I say, with intentional calm. "I know his tastes are standard, or slightly better than standard, better than his father's. He wants to do well." I shrug.

"You aren't listening."

"Go on."

"He's not a bad person, just confused, like a boy. Armenian men are boys. It's probably his father's fault he's insecure, caught between worlds. He will beat you because he will have to prove he is right . . ."

"Beat me? I don't understand."

"Beat you, yes. You don't think of it this way, but he does. He thinks of everything he does as winning and losing. He is going to win the project for two people: himself and himself in the eyes of his father."

"So if he wins, we win, right?"

"Not if he falls back on his father's expectations. We'll be asked to design something we won't believe in."

"I guess you've seen one of his father's hotels?"

"The soul of these buildings is to negate the possibility of having a soul." Nadia raises two fingers from each hand to place quotation marks around soul.

I stifle a laugh and at the same time I sense the chasm, again. Now it opens wider. My work is senseless . . .

"But, Mr. Moscowitz." She sighs.

The way she says "Mr. Moscowitz," with a sigh of irony, distracts me for a moment. I resist telling her of a recurring dream, crossing a stream or climbing a wall or ladder. As the dream plays on, I often slip, or something will distract me. A shoe will disappear. My pant leg will rip. I'll get into a long, senseless conversation. I might simply lose my glasses. I'll no longer be able to see where I'm going. I'll search and search for them, but I'll forget why, or even what I'm doing.

"As a practical matter," says Nadia, "in order for Mr. Terzian to review the drawings before the community meeting, we need to submit them August 6."

"Not the 15th."

"In other words—"

"In other words, what?"

"The clock is ticking."

9

THE NEXT DAY is Saturday. I wake up to a boy's voice. He is yelling, what? Something in rhythm. A metronomic bird in the cherry tree echoes his sweetly intense voice. How many boys like this one have grown up on this block of Aspen Street? For a waking moment, mental passages clear and clean, I manage some math. Forty row houses, two boys (a conservative average, considering the Irish Catholic heritage of the neighborhood) per house, from 1870 to 1970, about five generations. Eighty times five equals four hundred boys plus, on average, fewer per house 1970 to the present, say one per house, forty per generation, for two and a half generations. That equals another one hundred boys, making five hundred all together, which seems like many, and at the same time very few.

Of five hundred boys, I can distinguish the voices of five, in addition to the main boy, who goes on instructing the other boys about where they should throw the ball. The boy's name is Devon; to adults he is exceedingly polite. Now his voice lingers so that even when the voices and the footsteps of the other boys stop, for example to allow the number forty-eight bus to pass as it threads narrowly through the parked cars, or for a parent to remind one of them he has a haircut at two o'clock, I can still hear his voice with its avian intensity, imprinted on my memory. For a moment, still in the false clarity of early consciousness, I ask myself why the sound waves disappear, and if it might be possible to detect the particular voice of each of the five hundred boys who have grown up on this block layered one upon the other.

If buildings can account for bodies in the present, do they have a responsibility to the past? How can those voices be heard? Behind these questions another approaches, gingerly, as pooled water appears to hesitate before circling to the drain: If I give up the commission, can the office make it through the year? A stupid question, at second thought. If I give up the commission I will have to close. I will have to lay off Nadia.

I get up, finally, and shave. I wash my face, my eyes the green of fresh acorns. I put on a white T-shirt. On the day a man dies, it occurs to me while pulling on a light pair of pants, he dresses for the last time.

An hour after finishing my coffee, I start down the Parkway. I walk, as an Englishman in Cairo, in the center beneath the trees. Children are already swimming in the fountain in Logan Square. This time I notice mothers, grandmothers, uncles, coolers of beer, plates of chicken—as if the fountain really is a public swimming pool. I can't tell if this is wonderful or horrible. At City Hall I give in and take the subway to 5th Street, then walk diagonally through the throng of tourists sweltering on the wide lawn in front of Independence Hall. On 6th Street, several blocks south, construction closes the sidewalk toward Bainbridge Street. A sloppy chain-link fence protrudes halfway into the street. I have to cross to go around, or go down the alley, but that, too, is blocked. I spot Lyle Thomas, graying beard, hale pink cheeks, forgettable architect of school additions and reception stations, coming the other way, on the opposite side of 6th Street in front of the crêperie Beau Monde. I turn my back to the street and squint through the fence. I grab hold as if I'm climbing a sheer cliff. "Moscowitz! Moscowitz!" Lyle Thomas has a backroom voice; it emits without reflection. "The sky is falling, Moscowitz," he offers, a stupid joke meant to get my attention. With my shoulder I pretend to scratch an itch on my cheek. A bicyclist nearly brushes my shirt and I turn my head toward the street. A truck stops, as if to let me cross, but instead I'm frozen. Sweat gathers at my temples.

The building inside the fence has been an antiques mart, now I recall. Reginald once found a vintage jacket here, in the basement. It smelled like rose water. The antiques mart was inside an old synagogue, and now the synagogue will be something else, probably an apartment house. Another old synagogue, one of the five, including Love of Mercy, around my apartment building site. Buildings turn, like people do. They become other things.

On that Yom Kippur in 1889, Moskovitz wears a prayer shawl while he humiliates the religious men. The act, I imagine, has been meant to taunt. To hurt, to make fun: so that they will betray themselves by violating the holiest day of the year. But then it is also wickedly defiant. Standing there while they surround him in their righteous outfits, the same shroud of purity that he wears, too. But then he doesn't stop the police, who may already think of Jews as monsters, from arresting them. What makes a man punish other men? Demean them? Cut them down? And what, these pious must wonder, have they done to cause the wrath of God? Do those men feel shame before God for ending up in a damp prison cell, blaming Moskovitz for their misfortune? Cursing him and then having to ask God's forgiveness? Begging the police captain, who probably can't understand a word they are saying. Arrest that man! He's the cause of our trouble!

Are any of these men naturalized citizens? Nowadays they would be afraid of being deported.

Louis Moskovitz standing outside Love of Mercy has shamed himself. This is what the pious must say. He is no Jew! But Moskovitz is a Jew who can't believe that God would allow injustice. So either there is no God, or the God that exists must be feared. Either way, if God isn't going to do it, or he doesn't exist, it's up to men to fight for justice for everyone, equality for all human beings. Perhaps Moskovitz is a Jew who thinks the only way to seek justice is to stop being a Jew. Perhaps anarchist doctrine has blinded him to his religion.

Yet, according to Boonin, soon after the Yom Kippur protest, Louis Moskovitz stops going to anarchist meetings and ultimately becomes the head of the Jewish burial society. Perhaps on that day outside Love of Mercy, while reciting the Johann Most superimposed over the holy day prayer, he can't help but read both texts at once. But what compels a man to turn?

The sun is high in the sky. Louis Moskovitz must have walked here too, perhaps contemplating what he did. Perhaps hungry or tired or overworked. When he turns to religion, which synagogue does he attend? Perhaps this one, with its handsome baroque form.

It is a striking building, with two copper onion domes. The new copper installed by the developer is too bright, too gaudy, but it will darken, like sugar caramelizing. I'm still standing between traffic and the construction fence. It isn't safe. Has Lyle Thomas passed? I can't hear his voice. I should cross to the other side but maybe he's still there. In this city everything presses in. No one has any room.

"What do you think, is there anything wrong with it?" Lyle is here in front of me. Now both of us are pressed between traffic and the construction fence.

The question startles. This is like him. He assumes I'm already part of the conversation in his head. "Wrong with what?" My voice of annoyance.

"Don't you see? What the worker is doing. Isn't this what

you've been staring at, the worker taking down the Jewish ornamentation? Is it desecration, do you think?"

I struggle to find words. "I'm not sure."

"If it was a store, a new owner of a store taking down the old sign, putting up his new one, no one would care or question." Apparently Lyle is already deep into this conversation, probably with himself.

"I'm not sure." I try to focus on the worker. He's balanced on a ladder. Whoever is in charge of the work hasn't bothered to install a scaffold. The worker is wiry, unlike the thickly built Moskovitz, who stands like the trunk of a tree. This man doesn't look like a construction worker. He's wearing sneakers. At first I can't tell what he's doing. A car honks at us and I suck in my belly. Up on the ladder, the worker is using a power chisel to remove the Hebrew writing over the door. Now I realize that he's already ground off the Jewish stars on either side. It appears as if he's scabbed the building's skin, leaving a permanent, angry scar. I say so to Lyle Thomas.

"You think erasing is wrong?"

I shrug. "We should get out of traffic. This is a dangerous spot."

"They should have to put in a walkway."

"There's no room!" I raise my voice. "The problem is there's no room!" Somehow I get away.

Business is brisk at Terzian's parking lot. Cars are backed up on Bainbridge Street. Armen Terzian will leave the lot open until the last minute, until the earthmovers line up to come in. A reporter for the *Inquirer*, picking up on the *Daily News*'s profile of Arshad Terzian, has traced a pattern. Wealthy immigrants living in English-style estates on the Main Line are significant buyers of early American art, especially patriotic work by Peale and his sons, and Sully, Stuart, Trumbull, and the like. The *Inquirer* prints another photograph taken through a doorway of Arshad Terzian's manor, of Peale's full-length George Washington. Armen Terzian, the reporter lets out, accompanies his father to art auctions. The article seems to indicate, without doing so directly, that Armen, age thirty-eight, still lives at home.

Nadia is making progress with Terzian's apartment house. Late the day before, she suggested aligning the ground floor with the buildings on either side while angling the upper floors to increase solar gain. "At the very least it must do this," I said, without elaborating.

"What do you mean, 'at the very least'?"

"I mean just what I mean. You've set a baseline for the design. And now you'd like me to work with that, I presume?"

"If you don't like this idea, just say so."

"It's the baseline—"

"Do you want me to elaborate on it?"

"Yes, probably."

"Probably the design should be elaborated on or probably I should do it?"

How many times do Eva and I have this same twisted conversation? And still I have no satisfactory answer.

Inside the candy store at the end of Terzian's block, the man behind the counter smiles easily. Dark, curly hair rings a bald head; his glasses fall repeatedly down his nose. He pushes them up with his pinky, which extends at an odd angle. He's opposed to any more expensive housing in the neighborhood. "Rich people don't buy bags of gummy bears and candy worms," he says, laughing; "too unhealthy for their kids."

"Could be. I guess you would know. But aren't they the ones to indulge their precious ones, to say, 'a double scoop of ice cream is better than one.'"

"They'd be right about that!"

"So what would you want to see on the parking lot? More stores? An apartment house for not-too-wealthy eight-year-olds?"

He doesn't answer. He offers me a coffee. When I decline, he rests his head on his hands on top of the tall counter and

I sense now a troubled clown. "You guys don't know when to say when; you can't tell when you've gone too far," he says, repeating what must have been said to him, perpetually over-eager, all his life. Recognizing this, I forgive being lumped in among the shady real estate men, realtors, hack architects . . .

"All this 'luxury' stuff, it's kind of fake," he says. He lifts his head up and accidentally knocks his ring (of a coiled snake), on that same pinky finger, against the counter.

"I'm telling you this because you asked. Maybe you're different. Maybe you're a 'starchitect,' and I'm sure you know a lot more than I do. I'd rather leave that a shitty parking lot than—"

He cuts himself off and then smiles sadly. He offers imported chocolates; he offers local chocolates. Each time I say, "No, thanks." I think about my clichéd wide terraces and Nadia's passive solar gain. What could it mean to seek justice in architecture?

I cross the street, through the row of trees that have replaced the Washington Market, to Love of Mercy, handsome brownstone of effortless design. Here, Moskovitz stands in his prayer shawl under the market shambles that must have stretched almost all the way to the edge of the curb, just feet from the front steps of the synagogue, tortured by injustice, reciting his provocation to war.

10

Louis Moskovitz crouches over his grains, rearranging the display, fidgeting. I want to know if he opens shop the next day, the day after Yom Kippur. The religious return to work, assuming they have been freed from prison. But in the evening do they return to Love of Mercy? Now they have a reason to beg forgiveness. They have assaulted another man.

But what are we to think about that man? Has someone put him up to this stunt? I want to imagine that he is a true believer, standing up to the most powerful, the religious. Only later, when he is one of them, he becomes an actor playing a role, trying to prove he is worthy. Part of him must feel a fake.

The older you get, the more you feel that you are pretending anyway. As a young architect, I am sure of myself, certain I understand every dynamic, convinced I have the right design vision. I can see things others can't. In reality I am blind—or rather, I haven't yet learned how to look. My sight is developing. Yet, perhaps now when it should be clear, it isn't. Should I abandon architecture, I would spend my time this way, in pursuit of invisible lives.

"The majority of us didn't have a clear idea what we wanted, other than the fact that we were all atheists," writes Chaim Weinberg in *Forty Years in the Struggle: The Memoirs of a Jewish Anarchist*. On Sunday, I find Weinberg's history online, on a website called "Dead Anarchists." The goal of "Dead Anarchists," at least according to Robert Helms, who edits the site, is to trace the invisible lives to feed the imagination of present-day radicals. I'm tracing one, Moskovitz, across the streets of his neighborhood, in search of myself.

What is going through the mind of Louis Moskovitz as he stands at the edge of the shambles on Yom Kippur 1889? How does the city record this life, how does it know or remember him? The shambles are gone now, but the proximity of the market and the synagogue remains, the intimacy of space. If the windows are open, he can hear the religious pray in unison, the movement of their bodies, the rustling of their books, soles, the heels of their shoes against the wooden floor, the creak of the pews. They are pews from an old church, I imagine, and purchased by the men from Shavel on discount. The churchmen have no use for them anymore.

What is in the autumn air, in the Jewish quarter that Yom Kippur? Subversive words, words from other cities, from London and Paris and further east, from Berlin, from Vienna, from Moscow, soaking into Philadelphia mouths. Words carried on immigrant ships, words that pass inspection hidden inside the twisted mouths of sickly men and women, on their twisted tongues. In the infection, the words become twisted. The cigar factory isn't a feudal estate, but subjugation is the same, even if the owner of the factory is an immigrant, too, fortunate enough to have arrived sooner. The subjugated become the subjugators. It takes less than a generation. In reality, the words are twisted already, even before they arrive. Collectivism and anarchism, like lapping vines, curl inside each other. They intertwine. Johann Most is a socialist, a Marxist then anarchist then anarchist communist. He is a radical atheist. In 1882 he brings his words to America, the most dangerous of them: propaganda of the deed. "The existing system will be quickest and most radically overthrown by the annihilation of its exponents."

11

MORRIS RITTENBERG, a tailor, hosts the first meetings of the atheists in the Jewish quarter, says Boonin, the historian. As I start reading again on Monday morning, I text Nadia to say I'll be in late. She doesn't respond.

The 1875 atlas, left open in the browser, rushes across my computer screen. There is no synagogue yet across from the market shambles. The building it will replace, next to the dispensary (which is still labeled on the map in 1895), is the Howard Mission, and on the other side of that, a burial ground. I scroll past the Howard Mission, past the stables, past the Odd Fellows Hall, past a tiny alley called Hortsman's Row and Concord Street to Mr. Rittenberg's house. Does Louis Moskovitz attend these meetings? It seems likely. Harry Boonin says it is on this block that, on the night of Yom Kippur 1889, anarchists hold the Yom Kippur Ball. About one hundred people pay twenty-five cents for herring sandwiches and beer.

Voltairine de Cleyre is twenty-three when she arrives in Philadelphia that year, 1889. She is a Free Thinker, feminist, anarchist—a quiet, pretty, determined woman. "She herself had an ascetic kind of beauty. And she smelled very good, like lavender." Voltairine de Cleyre teaches English to Yiddish-speaking immigrants from the Pale of Settlement. Many are anarchists. One of them is Joseph Cohen. When Cohen and his wife come to de Cleyre's apartment on North Marshall Street, they bring their daughter, Emma, who sits on the teacher's lap during the lesson. It is Emma who notices the lavender scent. For sound and diction, de Cleyre uses the poems of Edgar Allan Poe, some written a few blocks from her apartment.

We must imagine Moskovitz, too, in de Cleyre's apartment, perhaps a little frightened by the teacher's direct gaze, expectant voice, by the "elegance" of her things. She demands he return the gaze and in that moment he becomes, at twenty-two or twenty-five, a man. "In those twelve years that I have lived and loved and worked with foreign Jews I have taught over a thousand, and found them, as a rule, the brightest, the most persistent and sacrificing students, and in youth dreamers of social ideals." De Cleyre writes these words in 1903, in an essay, "The Making of an Anarchist":

Cold, starvation, self-isolation, all endured for years in order to obtain the means for study; and, worse than all, exhaustion of body even to emaciation—this is common.

If Moskovitz is at the Ball, he must see his teacher there. She must inspire him with her simple stare. The next morning he will act. It isn't hard to imagine that he walks directly from the Ball to his market stand, which must open early in the morning. Past the Odd Fellows Hall, past the stables, still in darkness to Chevra Ahavath Chesed, morning ablutions under way.

I follow Boonin's footnote, number one hundred forty-nine: "These idealists . . . caused the worst kind of destruction—the tearing out of the heart."

For a while that year, Rittenberg the tailor hosts the meetings of the idealists at his small house. The building is two stories with a third-floor attic and traditional dormer window now handsomely restored, according to Street View; unlike most of the other houses on the block, which have been altered and enlarged so as to mask the original architectural features and proportions or removed altogether, this one remains, appearing as it must have when the anarchists started to meet. Here, says Weinberg in his memoir, they organize the *Riter fun Frayhayt*, the Knights of Liberty. We have to assume the meetings are conducted in Yiddish, that vanishing language. We have to press that language onto the scene, like oxide onto molten glass.

I stare into Chaim Weinberg's face as it appears on the cover of *Forty Years in the Struggle*, made distant through the grain of the old black-and-white photograph, digitized. Semitic eyes to shade the desert sun, cheeks pressed in by hunger, by kicks to the face. The host of the meetings, Rittenberg, Weinberg says, is blessed with five daughters. "Five daughters for a Jew: this alone would have been a misfortune, even if they had been personable and good-looking." Weinberg, undoubtedly, does not get along well with Voltairine de Cleyre, the feminist. He goes on: "Mr. Rittenberg had to have a doubly good fortune, five daughters, each one uglier than the next." I'm not sure I can get used to the brittle humor. Weinberg is writing in the 1930s. He can barely walk. He raises chickens. He has given up making cigars. From time to time, he gives a fiery speech to a trade union, tempering fire with dreams of a collective bakery or a collective housing project. "This Mr. Rittenberg, however," he continues, "understood the business; how could he more easily marry off his five 'beauties' than in this circle where the people were more preoccupied with ideas and plans for the future than with the reality on earth? And in truth, he was not mistaken. He managed to give away all five, and, of course, after that we never saw his face again."

Weinberg makes obsessive note of those, like Rittenberg, who abandon the movement, apostates. The accounting is apocryphal. The laughter is bitter. Moskovitz—Moscowitz as the name translates in Weinberg's text—isn't spared. He also isn't Louis. "Isidore Prenner . . . Julius Moscowitz, Morris Gillis, and Louis Jacobs were arrested on the evening of October 11, 1891 for incitement to riot at a meeting at 512 South 3rd Street, 3rd floor."

12

JULIUS MOSCOWITZ: now the spellings of our family names match, according to Weinberg, that stub-faced agitator, always suffering from lack of respect. Moscowitz—shall I keep using Moskovitz, just to keep us separate? No, I'll follow Weinberg's spelling, even if it's an accident of translation. He knows the man, at least so he says. And the man, according to Weinberg, is now involved in a second Yom Kippur protest, this one two years after the incident in front of Love of Mercy.

But which Moscowitz? Now I'm worried there are two: one who is a radical and one who is religious. These can't be the same man. Weinberg is confused. Weinberg seems to me someone who might be easily confused. Maybe history can split you in two.

Or maybe history can condense you into one.

"What is it about this commission?" demands Nadia when I show up at the office in the afternoon. "It's turning you into someone else. You don't work anymore. It's like you can't focus, like nothing matters."

I try to hide my gaze.

She decides to prod. "I've completed the massing study . . ."

"I don't need reminding."

"No, I completed it. Terzian's assistant keeps calling . . . And suggesting a meeting at their office in the suburbs. There's already a pile of pink message slips on your desk."

"We'll be ready," I say.

In Nadia's presence, my ambivalence seems doubly foolish. Had she been with me in the candy shop . . .

"You're working on the floor plans," she continues.

"___"

"Yes or no?"

"It isn't so simple . . ."

"My uncle used to say this same thing," she whispers. She doesn't want to believe I am falling apart. "And he would pretend to be bashful. He ended up in jail."

"What?"

"I learned observing him never to assume that something is what it seems."

When Nadia steps away, I do something rare, probably unprecedented. I shut the door to my office.

Weinberg, in his memoir, is fond of noting the address or corner where events take place, as if to say to the reader in the 1930s, or even the present day, "The city isn't always what the city seems." Thus we learn about the building at 512 S. 3rd Street, now the most elegant and enchanting building on its block, where Moscowitz is arrested the evening of October 11, 1891, during the second Yom Kippur Ball. Further detail is found in the footnotes. A radical immigrant couple from Galicia, in the Pale of Settlement, Dr. Max Staller and his wife, Jennie Magul Staller, act in theater productions at 512 S. 3rd put on by the Star Specialty Club. Performances are going on in 1891 when Moscowitz is arrested. A split-off anarchist group, the Pioneers of Liberty, meets here, too. Dr. Staller, along with other anarchist physicians, opens the Mt. Sinai Dispensary at 236 Pine Street, around the corner, a few years later. I imagine Robert Helms, the editor of "Dead

Anarchists," writing these footnotes. He has also written a short book, *George Brown, the Cobbler Anarchist of Philadelphia*, which I find at the Wooden Shoe, an anarchist bookstore on South Street. Harry Boonin, too, faithfully aligns events and buildings. His book might be called an historical atlas. It's organized according to street.

In his biography of George Brown, Helms describes Brown as one of the anarchist leaders of Philadelphia in the 1890s. So is Weinberg, he says, and four women: Natasha Notkin, Brown's partner Mary Hansen, Moscowitz's teacher Voltairine de Cleyre, and Margaret Perle McLeod. In winter 1892, soon after Moscowitz's arrest, McLeod begins hosting meetings of the Ladies Liberal League at her house at 218 S. 8th Street, where she has also made room for the Radical Library, a workers' reading room, open each night 8–10 p.m.

To commit to the movement means living with messianic fervor.

I glide around on my office computer. Street View takes me from 218 S. 8th Street to 236 Pine. I overshoot corners, reverse, tilt up, circle around. From Pine up to 3rd, from 3rd to Catherine. Gliding is faster than walking. The city rushes by, backwards. I go east toward the original streets of the city and therefore back in time. Perhaps 240 Catherine Street, Rittenberg's house, is the oldest of the four, but nothing in the city happens in sequence. A city is the product of simultaneous urges.

These four buildings, 512 S. 3rd, 218 S. 8th, 236 Pine, and 240 Catherine, have been stripped of age. Perhaps coincidentally, they form a set. Clean brick, brilliant black trim and shutters, restored woodwork, arched doorways, Palladian window lights. The façade of McLeod's house has settled. You can see this at the roofline. The brick waves, the cornice sags. It appears that bolts have been inserted to set the façade in place. This is time recorded, but mute time, time that stakes no claim. The anarchists probably staked little claim to these buildings. They were useful, well located, perhaps in the case of 512 S. 3rd Street with its tall ceilings, accommodating. Moscowitz is arrested there in 1891; later, does he come to resent this block?

Back to 3rd Street on my computer screen. The Pioneers of Liberty, *Pionire der Frayhayt*, in the transliterated Yiddish spoken by Moscowitz and his comrades, are holding their Yom Kippur Ball here on October 11, 1891. To repent one's sins, one must reject worldly things, and so Yom Kippur is a night and day of fasting. Yet to liberate themselves, they must reject their religion. The anarchists will eat and drink all night and day in lavish celebrations. But by rejecting Yom Kippur, instead of simply ignoring it, they also admit to being bound, like anyone tied to religious tradition.

This is the wrestling that's going on on the second floor of 512 S. 3rd Street when the cops bust in. What comes to mind is a scene from Charlie Chaplin: a pair of undistinguished cops, their hats too large for their heads, knock on the door, knock again, wait a moment, step back, and then, hearing troubling words through the open upstairs window, take a hatchet to the locked door. All the world depends on ending this menace. Upstairs, in a room cluttered with swarthy faces, a woman with a short haircut gives a fiery speech as an impressionable young woman looks on. A young man— cunningly handsome, but with a dirty, torn coat—who has brought the young woman to the Ball, takes a swig from his beer, smiles at her, revealing bad teeth (and therefore bad intentions). Just then the policemen begin the raid. Chaplin empathizes with the poor radicals, of course. One of them, idealistic and humble, in an effort to save the young woman from prison, grabs her and steals her out through the fire escape. Will they make it?

The building stares back at me. Someone has restored the cast-iron storefront, the tall window arches, delicate brickwork; someone has made this building speak, but I'm afraid it doesn't remember the *Pionire der Frayhayt*. It has lost the Yiddish. It just won't say.

Harry Boonin, in his history of the neighborhood, recalls a time when Hebrew letters, two and three feet high, are painted on the façades of buildings in the Jewish quarter. In a circa 1910 photograph, two graybeards stand before the Old People's Home and a welcome bureau for newcomers. Pants cinched at the waist and hands in his pockets, the man on the right stands between the other man and a wooden electrical pole, as if they are three vagrants lined up for the camera. The pole, with its heavy wires and cross beams and insulated couplings, is ugly and obtrusive, like the immigrant Jews perhaps, but also a welcome miracle of progress. So it is written on the building: הכנסת ארחים. Boonin says this means "Hospitality to Strangers."

Across the open book on my desk, Boonin brushes ghost Hebrew letters on the façade of 512 S. 3rd. In 1896, Meyer Sharshik, from "Russian Poland," purchases the building where Moscowitz is arrested. This is four-plus years after the Yom Kippur Ball arrest. In Russia, Sharshik is known as Beryl Zeitchik. In America, like Moscowitz, he is a peddler, "a pack on his back from early morning." In 1887, two years before Moscowitz the peddler performs his first anarchist prayers on Yom Kippur, Zeitchik-Sharshik opens a warehouse store to sell merchandise to peddlers. Sharshik's creditors say, "Sell him only for cash & do not recommend him in any other way." Boonin has found this quote in a credit report in the library archive of Harvard University. Perhaps it is a form of blanket anti-Semitism.

Does Sharshik sell Moscowitz his peddler supplies? Is the peddler Moscowitz named Louis or Julius? The anarchist or the religious?

The buildings are in the text, the people in the footnotes. I return to Louis Moskovitz, peddler, standing in front of Love of Mercy in 1889. The story comes from a book in Yiddish, *Di Yidish-Anarkhistishe Bavegung in Amerike,* by Joseph Cohen, former student of Voltairine de Cleyre. The book is from 1945. Maybe Louis is a mistranslation. Moskovitz is Moscowitz, it makes no difference. When the book arrives in the mail the next afternoon from an online bookseller, I show it to Nadia. She lingers over a stamp on the cover page, "Women's Club of San Francisco—Workman's Circle Br. 806."

Her face is oily from the heat.

"Sold to Mrs. Papick." Pah-peek, she says. "If Mrs. Papick bought this book, why did someone write that in it?"

"Maybe she wrote it herself to remember her name."

"The stamp and the woman's name are an imprint, a marking," says Nadia, answering her own question. "It's so old and still it's almost permanent."

In two hours the translator I find on the Internet, working from photos of a few pages of the original book in Yiddish, returns a couple solid pages of English text. When Moskowitz—now we have a third spelling—opens his stand on Yom Kippur, writes Cohen in the English translation, he "inadvertently plays a trick on them." The word "inadvertently": has the peddler merely intended a private protest? He hasn't expected customers, says Cohen. Now Moskovitz-Moscowitz-Moskowitz appears in pure light, a simple believer (and a believer in one thing can switch his beliefs if he likes). He is heroic. But his presence alone causes the religious to lose their minds. In New York almost a decade later, the Herrick brothers, owners of a delicatessen on Division Street, decide to stay open during Yom Kippur. Their decision isn't inadvertent. The open restaurant, filled with diners, Jews and Gentiles, reads like a taunt. Several thousand react instinctively. They snap. They surround the deli in a struggle for sanctity. A struggle for tradition. America will eat anything. It will eat your fast day too. The Herrick brothers are socialists, "at the same time Hebrews and Socialists," reports the *New York*

Times on September 27, 1898. The mob is after a two-headed monster. "They were not open to the argument that fighting might be as bad as eating on such a day, and, as a result, the police had their hands full."

So standing outside Love of Mercy in autumn 1889 Moscowitz has baited the men inside. But is he responsible for their behavior? Cohen writes that Louis Moskowitz, with the religious men closing in on him, "feigned innocence." If you knowingly lure someone into a trap of self-betrayal, does it matter who shuts the door?

After that, "the religious Jews had it out for this Moskowitz." They hold a grudge from the incident at Love of Mercy in 1889. They feel that he is to blame for their arrest. Two years later, the religious Jews accuse Louis Moskowitz of giving "dangerous and inciting" speeches while handing out pamphlets advertising the Yom Kippur Ball. Why can't they let it go?

Moskowitz, they say, has been struck blind with fervor.

Weinberg says the same religious Jews claimed that while pamphleting Julius Moscowitz attacked a "gray-haired Jew and hit him with a set of *tefillin*, of all things."

I want to know, in the process of translating Yiddish to English, could the name Julius be confused with Louis? The translator responds by email: "I don't know of any obvious connection between the names Louis and Julius, but how many former anarchists who went on to become head of the Chevra Kadisho (literally, the Holy Society) could there have been?"

13

"NICK," SAYS ARMEN TERZIAN, "I don't care about the past."
His voice is quiet and cold. I find it attractive. We shake
hands in the center of the parking lot, near the guardhouse.
What he means is the last few weeks, the miscommunication
and slow response from my office. Perhaps he isn't like his
father, or at least the caricature of Arshad Terzian presented
in the papers. No, why should he be? Nadia has exaggerated
the power his father has over him. Perhaps in Beirut she knew
an Armenian family . . . Why didn't I press her to explain
more? Armen is a mild man. Mild: the word keeps asserting
itself. He lives at home.

I want to grab Terzian's forearm gently but forcefully to
tell him about Moskowitz, Louis or Julius it doesn't matter,
a man who comes here, too, and marks his territory. I don't
grab Terzian's forearm but I see myself doing it so vividly I
sense I am hallucinating. In the hallucination, Terzian doesn't
try to break free. He listens to my story with his head down.

I tell him instead about the detailed research Nadia has
been doing. I mention the massing studies, one at four sto-

ries, another at five, yet another at six. I see myself waving my hands for emphasis.

"When will I see something real?" His voice is pointed all of a sudden. His shave is clean and close.

"The practice of architecture . . ." I take a moment to look him in the eyes. Mild, still. I take the upper hand. "I think you underestimated the timeline, what's involved. I said right away the timeline made me nervous."

"I don't recall that."

"Nevertheless—"

He lowers his voice to a whisper. "Look, I'm not the same as my father," he says. He waits for me to shuffle uncomfortably, pats his forehead with a handkerchief, and firms his stance. "He has a formula and that made my family rich. But I don't want to do the same thing over and over. That doesn't interest me."

"OK."

"So, if we can figure out this one—if you can give me something everyone will love, and they give us the five or six stories, then let's get to work. I like to learn."

August 6 is ten days away. If I meet the deadline . . . then there will be future commissions, bigger, better, presumably. It isn't clear to me why people do things. "I like to learn," he says. He also says he wants a design "everyone will love." These are opposite instincts.

It's true that my office has no commissions to follow this one. It's true I'm not sure I want any. I've left Nadia exposed. By keeping her working in my office, aren't I asking her to betray her best interests? She should move to another firm.

"You seem confused about what I'm offering."

I smile. "No, sir—that's quite clear." Before he gets back inside his Audi I reassure him he'll have what he needs August 6.

Reginald and I stand here one night not long after the protest against the expansion of the oil refineries along the river—late at night, the spotlights towering over us, everything deserted. For some reason you can't hear the noise of South Street. The light shines on the emptiness, and we, two friends since the first day of college, are having it out. Who will pay for the parking? We don't usually park here, but earlier there were no spaces on the street. Eva is in the car. I ask her if she has money. She reminds me we used the last of it for "those really great fries." Reginald says he will go get money, there has to be a bank machine nearby. For some reason he walks south, away from South Street. The last we see him, he is facing the Love of Mercy synagogue (I superimpose this detail) and then we lose him in the dark.

Just the same, I imagine the parking lot disappearing from the city. Maybe I should want to cover over the memory of that night. All these years I've run from it, not just that night, but the tortured last months of our affair, of our youth, and what I did . . . and what I didn't do. Now I feel I must try to remember. Well, it doesn't matter. I don't need the parking lot to recall those last months, the fierce distance and then the need in her eyes, the fear in mine.

That night in the parking lot, Eva's glasses fog when she grabs me into the car and we huddle up against the cold. Silence, comrade of the cold and the dark, pushes in. Eva kisses my neck. Her lips are warm and tender, but I am sleepy. She lowers her head to my chest, but between us coats buckle and gather. "My head is spinning," she says, finally.

"I'm sorry," I respond, aimlessly. Then: "How did you know I'd agree to ending the pregnancy?"

She buries herself deeper and sighs—she doesn't want to talk about it.

I mutter something unintelligible about rights—she has a claim to them, of course. And yet we might have discussed it.

"When you ejaculate, you let go."

"Maybe."

"No! You forfeit."

The car is claustrophobic. I stretch just slightly for air and she follows, burrowing deeper, digging in and pulling away both at once.

"Reg took me. You don't know that. Now you do."

"Now I do . . ."

"Sometimes he is there for me and not for you."

A police car's red and blue lights seep through the back window of Reginald's Corolla, making it seem like the car has begun to glow from the inside, like a deep sea organism articulating fear. Eva looks up into the hot light reflecting off the rearview mirror, and for a moment it's as if her face is in negative light, like an x-ray. And for that moment, I see her hardening into someone else.

"Where is Reg?" she says, idly.

"He's lost forever." I rest my head against the cold window. How can I make sense of this person who is so decisive and yet is constantly demanding I become more accepting of contradiction? That seems like a contradiction itself.

"Fully empirical," she says, somehow picking up the earlier conversation about rights and responsibility. "If I didn't let go of my parents," she says, "and their absurd lifestyle, and even my own memories of it, I could never be honest with myself and see life as possibility, but that isn't based on a lesson or a theory or an answer, it's based on openness."

"—"

"Shh, Nicholas, letting go isn't the same as shutting down. Open the window, I can't breathe."

"He has no sense of direction," I say.

"I picture him lost in one of those junkyards—where are those junkyards?"

"Under the Passyunk bridge."

"He won't survive it. He is afraid of dogs."

"Wherever he's gone, it's for a reason."

"See, my parents let me play field hockey and go to normal school because they knew I would have to get it for myself."

We fall asleep until Reginald returns, banging at the window. He's gotten cash and also another person. She is attractive and has a high-pitched voice and follows him into the car, which I drive, navigating through Queen Village, past the Southwark housing project, eyes like x-ray beams on pavement, across Passyunk, across Broad Street and along Washington Avenue. I swerve unconsciously on the Grays Ferry Bridge.

Armen Terzian opens his window halfway just before he pulls away from me standing in the parking lot. "I want this building to turn heads," the real estate man says, almost bashfully. An architect hears these words in a dream. He whispers them to himself. He denies they are possible. I am like a blind man handed pages of scripture. The most authentic response I have when, later in the afternoon, I sit at my computer is to line up some concepts, none of them original, and enter them as if keywords into CAD. Movement. Tactile. Permeable. Sustainable. Natural. Provocative. Hit enter. Everything is borrowed and nothing is real.

14

THE ELEVATOR is the defining advance of the second half of the nineteenth century. First it is used to move coal. Then people. At the Crystal Palace, Otis demonstrates it can be done. Technology guides the architect's hand. It isn't me working but an aspirational engineer. He says a person doesn't need stairs to go from floor to floor and thus he is free; he can go farther than his feet can take him. The architect is free to build as tall as he wants, as tall as the structural engineer says he can.

In 1887 a man named Alexander Miles gets a patent for elevator doors that will close automatically. Miles lives in Duluth, Minnesota. You won't accidentally fall through the shaft because of Alexander Miles. The elevator, with its safety doors, is the object of fascination in 1892. Pages and pages of the city directory that year advertise elevators with safety doors. I'm looking at the city directory on microfilm in the library, in a room that has the exact proportions of a fish tank. It is humid outside, the air like brine. After walking here from the office, I struggle to breathe.

Microfilm uncoils. The sound it makes is like static, like

searching for a station. In the library I am absorbed in anachronism. The wooden chairs are almost too heavy to move. Scoot the chair forward to dive closer to the names in the directory backlit through yellow gossamer film and the chair against floor spits out a screech like television interference. In the tank of anachronism the occupations of the men listed in the city directory—almost all are men—peddler, fixer, huckster, "segarmkr"—seem perfectly natural.

Pogroms let loose these people, if we trace back. In the time of Napoleon, of *War and Peace*, Russia gains its empire, carves out Poland, Romania, Lithuania, Galicia, Ukraine, Belarus. Gains Jews. Forces them south, restricts their movement, traps them in fields and peasant villages, the Pale of Settlement. Holds them in side-glance. Allows some to grow in economic stature, to taste assimilation, to feel *Russian*. If there is Jewish original sin it must be this, to imagine she belongs. It takes only the slenderest rumor, when Tsar Alexander II is assassinated (by atheists, but not Jewish atheists), to lay blame on the Jews.

By the late 1880s, the Jewish surnames in the city directory begin to thicken, as I see on the microfilm screen. Morris, Mortimer, Mort, Moser, Moses . . . the static is parting. On the imagined TV dial the call letters dance. The letters of my name. Moscovitzs, Moskovitz, Moscourtz, Moskowitz, Moscovitz, Moschkowitz, Moskovitch, Muskovitz, Moskovisch, Moskowitch, Moscewitz. Abraham Moskovitz, at 612 S. 4th Street, across the street from our bar, where I encounter Reginald and Eva the last time, runs a variety store. This is 1886. In 1887, at the same address, he sells matches. In 1888 his name is spelled Moscovitz. He sells watches. Now a tattoo parlor operates in the building. "Tiki Tatoo." Someone has painted a Polynesian scene to cover the façade. A woman in a grass skirt, a beach circled with palm trees. The upstairs windows are covered. The woman is ten feet tall. She appears to be beckoning the gods.

In 1888, there is Lepold Moscovitz, a clerk two doors down from the watch store, and Loeb Moscowitz on Bainbridge Street, but no Louis or Julius. In 1891, the year of the second Yom Kippur Ball, no Louis or Julius. 1892 is the first year that either name appears; they both do. Julius Moskovitz is a tailor at 429 Carpenter Street, about six blocks south of Love of Mercy synagogue. Louis Moskowitz is a clerk at 257 N. 9th Street. Louis's address is far from the Jewish quarter. This suggests that Julius is the correct first name of the anarchist who later becomes the president of the Holy Society. But, according to Weinberg, in 1892, Julius is in jail.

In 1893, Moscowitzes of various spellings are barbers, tailors, brush makers, grocers, peddlers, tinsmiths, cigar makers, and clerks; they sell clothing, hats, trimmings, and shoes. Julius and Louis are both listed that year, still on Carpenter Street and North 9th Street, respectively, doing the same work as the year before.

The next year, Julius Moskovitz, still a tailor, has remained on Carpenter Street, but now Louis sells hats on North 8th Street. I note something else: he lists his home address as 643 South Street, in the Jewish quarter. I notice that I've forgotten where I am.

Julius is a tailor. Louis sells hats in a millinery store. Neither is a peddler. So who is? In 1888, one year before the first Yom Kippur confrontation at Love of Mercy synagogue, Loeb Moscowitz lists himself as a peddler living at 4 r 640 Bainbridge Street. He doesn't appear again until 1891, but now as Leon. "Moscovitz Leon, peddler h r 642 Bainbridge" ("h" indicates this is his home, "r" means rear). On the street atlas of 1895, 640 and 642 Bainbridge Street are represented as one single building, shaped like an L. Transforming and disappearing as the buildings he inhabits, Loeb/Leon lists his address as 4 r 642 Bainbridge. It's likely he lives in a worker's house called a trinity, accessible from an alley. A trinity has a single room on each floor. It is three stories high.

I am beginning to doubt my earlier conclusion. Isn't it likely that Loeb/Leon would walk every day to his spot in the Washington Market, exactly three blocks away? Even on Yom Kippur . . .

Loeb/Leon doesn't appear in the directory again until 1894. Sure enough, now he tells the representative from James Gopsill's Sons, the publisher of the directory, that his name is Louis: Leon's address in 1891 and Louis's address in 1894 are the same. The missing years correspond to the time Louis is arrested during the Yom Kippur Ball, 1891 through his imprisonment. Weinberg says the trial begins in March 1892 and that Moscowitz serves eight months. Depending on the length of the trial, he may not go free until 1893. Cohen concludes his chapter on "The Anti-Religious Agitation": "Louis Moskowitz remained in Philadelphia. After his time in prison he became a respectable Jew," a new man.

"Moskowitz Louis, tailor, h 4 r 642 Bainbridge."

15

I AM TOGGLING AGAIN. 1875. 1895. 1910. 1934. Today. The 1875 atlas, in butter yellow, occupied buildings hashed, shows seven rear trinity houses at 642 Bainbridge accessible from Darcy Street, really an alley, only accessible from another alley. "Alley" is pejorative. This second alley is called Spafford Street. The cartographer gives out the label "street" with an air of aspiration. There is no indoor plumbing on Darcy Street in 1875, probably not in 1895. There is no room for a bathroom in a trinity. I click to 1934, an appraisal map. At broader scale it smothers the 1875 atlas. The breath of the 1934 appraisal map created by J. M. Brewer for the Metropolitan Life Insurance Company tastes of bile. Racial concentrations are noted in a *mala bandera* of red (colored), green (Italian), blue (Jewish). 642 Bainbridge, in 1934, is green. The Jewish quarter has shrunk, blue pushed back east of Fifth Street. Red burns the western edge.

A constellation of uppercase Ds and Es and DEs, in red ink, drift across the map. Redlining's code: A = Highest class,

B = Upper class, C = Middle class, D = Lower class, E = Decadent. "As a residential area values have been at a vanishing point for many years."

Louis Moskowitz's trinity has already vanished in 1934, the year the Federal Housing Administration begins redlining neighborhoods. What year were the rest of the buildings in the center of the block erased? I have trouble deciphering the maps. Did Louis push a cart down Darcy, down Spafford, down Bainbridge? Or did he go first to Meyer Sharshik for supplies?

The city keeps going forward and maybe it isn't any of my business.

The day, only eight weeks ago, when Terzian awarded me the commission for the apartment house, I asked him what had been on the parking lot. What year were they demolished? "I can guess," he replied.

Who can tell what's missing once it's gone?

The maps, at least, give us clues. What is there, on Terzian's parking lot, in 1934 (and certainly long before)? Four trinity houses, a warehouse, and some commercial buildings. They are lightly streaked with blue and red, as if to suggest only a minor infection of Jews and blacks, and labeled "C," middle class. An in-between space, a void, and now the dominion of cars. Nadia stands in the doorway to my office. Coffee, chestnut, cinnamon; something unleashes inside me, and I look away.

How will the ghost mapmaker label the block once Terzian's apartment house is complete? A, B, C, D, or E?

"Let's make a 'C' building," I say, when she sits down at the worktable in my office.

"What?"

"A 'C' building. Look."

She's never seen a redline map, the truth of America made plain. She looks at me as if to say, "This is interesting, but what does it have to do with our building?"

Her look turns from confusion to fear. It lands on worry. I feel her compassion, though I don't want to.

"Keep working out the passive solar issue," I say, and lean back in the chair, which gives with my weight.

"OK," she says, nodding.

"I have an idea for social spaces." The words are like empty orbs falling from the sky. "What if we intentionally design the building so that little children can run around?"

"Children? Does Terzian want children?"

What am I doing? Demarcating boundaries, forcing Nadia to act . . . For a moment a thought passes: Moskowitz deserves his assault.

When Nadia leaves, I click to the translation of Cohen's memoir. Weinberg, he writes, convinces him to become an anarchist. They are friends until 1934, the year of demarcating boundaries. In 1935 Weinberg loses his head over a woman who is trying to leave their collectivist farm. The group votes to return her some of her dues, $100; Weinberg excoriates her in a public speech for breaking up the unity of the community. Cohen attempts to moderate the dispute, costing him his friend of three decades. Weinberg removes Cohen from his memoir.

This must have taken Weinberg days with a red pen.

Weinberg, says Cohen, in the short passage returned to me by the translator, is one of the speakers on the night of October 11, 1891, the start of Yom Kippur called Kol Nidre, on the second floor of 512 S. 3rd Street. The other speakers are Isidore Prenner and Jacob Appel. When the police raid the party they are as bungling as I imagine them. They arrest Prenner and Morris Gillis. The arrest of Gillis is an accident—mistaken identity. "Instead of Weinberg, they arrested M. Gillis, who also limped on one leg, was also a cigar-maker, a bit of a speech-maker."

16

At NINETEEN, I start spelling my name with a k and a v. The sharp edges have a geometry, a visual accord. The letters feel more Russian. I strangely want to feel more Russian. During a class on modernist art, we study the Constructivists. It is possible and not only possible, necessary, to construct a new world based on new ideas and new forms—abstract ideas and forms that break free of history. This is the sort of student I am, at nineteen. The world is moving. Why aren't we moving with it? Now I feel the first stirrings of interest in architecture, because it is the construction of ideas. Walking around becomes reading and thinking.

I am filled with the certainty that I will in some way build a new world.

I am powerful but I'm not paying any attention, powerful only in my own head, and therefore distorted. I recognize this but at the same time there isn't anything I can do about it. I relieve the strange, sharp feeling by walking.

I have to explain to my professors that I've changed the letters in my name.

Reginald and I are heading toward the peace sign. For some reason we think it's noteworthy that such a sculpture exists. To sit near it confers some kind of significance. We cut through the mass of students instead of going around. The body at nineteen is magnetic. I step on something, nearly trip. A snap. What is it? Ah, someone's headphones. She is lying on her stomach, she doesn't see. She is reading *Critique of Pure Reason*. The headphones must be broken. Reginald doesn't realize anything has happened. He's still walking. Reginald more than me is hidden in his own distortion. This is his beauty. I say, "Wait."

I pick up the headphones, in two pieces. The plastic head strap is broken right through. I bend down. "Excuse me, I'm sorry," I say. She bends herself toward me, sleepy, hair in a half-loosened bun. "Oh, hi," she says, as if she knows me; I don't know her. Her eyes are cinnamon. "Look, I'm sorry, my friend accidentally stepped on your headphones," I say.

The words come out naturally. All the same I am stunned by my own insouciance. This is Eva. I offer to buy her a new set of headphones, but she shrugs and goes back to her book.

I don't apologize to Reginald or try to explain. I pretend that's what really has happened. Why doesn't he get angry?

Nadia returns to the doorway to my office. A new tack—get me to discuss something real. Have I heard anything about the removal of the Jewish iconography from the synagogue on 6th Street? She keeps seeing it on the architecture blogs. "Does it offend you?" she asks. She means as a Jew, do I feel attacked? I have to explain that I'm not a practicing Jew. "What does it matter, practicing or not? It's who you are. So doesn't it bother you?"

"Are you asking me if I think that somehow our building can account for the loss? Because I think it might."

She looks at me with disappointment and disgust.

"I become physically sick, looking at the photos," she says. The quiver in her voice startles me with its honesty. Exposed, she awakens me. In the moment I have to listen. She shows me one of the photographs of the Hebrew letters over the doorway. The long name of the synagogue,

בית הכנסת הגדולה דחברה בני ראובן אנשי ספרד נתידד שנת תרמז

—and the Hebrew declaration inside the two wreaths,

זה השער לד׳ צדיקים יבואו בו

—are being chiseled out. The entrance to the building no longer instructs, "This is the gate of the Lord, the righteous shall enter into it." The shadows that are left and the discoloration of the stone make the letters appear strangely gilded, but clouded, as if the gilder had a shaky hand. "Do you see what they did?" she asks. "Instead of leaving the letters in place and covering them over, they removed each one, one at a time. They did it very carefully, as if they were savoring this filthy task, or as if they were writing the words all over again, one letter at a time, but in negative, erasing as they were writing."

17

NADIA STARES, and the stare reminds me that her father once fought with the Fedayeen. You are looking for something else, her eyes say. Open me up, see what's inside, mine taunt. Inborn shame, like some kind of original, fundamental sin. I worry over cruelty. I must keep guard. So I stay silent.

We'll have to work all afternoon on the design of the apartment house. The vulnerability she expressed over the synagogue has provoked some kind of opposite reaction in me. I demand Nadia respond with solutions to the architectural problems I put forth. I press her for options on maximizing profit per square foot. I tell her I am thinking like Terzian, the developer. I am him! Why should I build this if it isn't going to make me enough money?

Nadia nods, as if to ignore me.

Then she turns and stands with hands fidgeting with her hair. And I sit, uncertain and confused.

Once, in the dining room at 417 S. 49th Street, at the wooden bakery table, Eva stands above me trying to explain Kierkegaard's notion of "repetition." It is Indian summer, but the cavernous house keeps the tile floor cool and my feet are bare. We have just read *Fear and Trembling* and now we have begun *Repetition*. This is the first time we have taken a class together, and it isn't going well. "You can't read Kierkegaard if you are looking for an answer," she says.

"Stop being repetitive," I answer.

Reginald, sitting at the other end of the table, looks up and says, "Evolution preordained this entire ludicrous conversation."

A month into the course and we are trying to understand what Kierkegaard says is the difference between *recollection* and *repetition*. I read aloud from the page where I am underlining, as a child hums words he has heard adults say, "'For hope is a beckoning fruit that does not satisfy; recollection is petty travel money that does not satisfy; but repetition is the daily bread that satisfies with blessing.'"

"Bread is always more valuable than petty travel money," says Reginald.

"Repetition means you have to keep trying," says Eva, "seeking faith, let's say, or God's love. It means the love will be repeated, but not only love, self-knowledge."

"__"

"But, listen, Nicholas. I think what Kierkegaard is saying is that love, which is supposed to lead to a lifetime of repetition of itself as a search for faith, gets negated if the lover, or lovers, transform the love into its romantic idea. The idea of love, or marriage, isn't the real thing." This is the first time she suggests that this is what I'm doing. But she's only revealing her own discomfort. It's too powerful, too much. She's trying to protect herself.

"Each concept in Kierkegaard contains itself and its opposite. Intimacy, for example, reveals distance."

Recalling this conversation, I am reminded that our relationship, at the moment we study Kierkegaard, begins to falter. We stop trying, day after day, to approach love. Is this my fault? Am I in love with the idea of love? In the days that follow we struggle with intimacy and distance and tell ourselves we're trying to work it out. It's impossible to tell this in our tiny bed, where she abandons reason, or even the capacity to reason, and often we fail to sleep. It's as if, growing up in the free-love colony, she's gleaned an extra body consciousness and presented me with the gift. Our bodies are opposite electric.

We are young, but since the moment I crushed her headphones, together we produce an eternal sexual energy, sweet and sad, heavy and light. I wonder if the house at 417 S. 49th Street has ever stopped feeling it.

Nadia leaves the office around 6:30, another day without resolution. Are we any closer to producing what Terzian needs on August 6? Gently she shuts the door. The gentleness reverberates inside me as if it is Eva's touch, her lips on my neck. Sometime later, I leave, too, and drift through the mounds of people in Rittenhouse Square. I can barely distinguish one person from the other. Walking slowly in the heat, it takes nearly an hour to reach Terzian's parking lot. It is still light and even hotter here. Near the Delaware, once, three or four hundred years ago, this was lowland swamp.

The unlit cobra-style street lamp on Bainbridge Street, attached to a telephone pole, swings in the stifling breeze. The lamp threatens to break off from the wooden pole and crash to the ground. I want to build up, to build a totem, not an apartment house. The totem will go down deep into the swamp and high up into the sky; only the totem can account for all the layers. Terzian still operates the parking lot, squeezing out every last penny. To park here, you drive over the in-filled remains of whom? You drive over them, you don't even feel it.

I stand in Moscowitz's spot in the Washington Market. "The market was removed long ago; in its place is a so-called little park and several dried up trees," says Cohen in his 1945 memoir. Boonin's book is in my hand, open to the page showing the synagogue after the fire in 1943. My gaze lifts from open book to the building in front of me and back to the book; not yet have I felt so close to Moscowitz, the synagogue breathing down on us in heavy intimacy, both of us with a need to pull things apart. For just a moment my head is his head, nodding from text to street, street to text. It must appear I am rehearsing a speech. The book is an extension of my hands and for a moment I don't feel my feet in the hesitant darkness. Cars glide by, but they aren't cars, they can't be cars. A flattened beer can rattles under a tire. I wait for footsteps and I close my eyes, but no one is coming. Doors slam, left then right. Jingle of keys.

Belief is blinding. I discover this when I look up. It isn't the synagogue of the people from Shavel before me; this isn't the same building. I lean against the pole, my book bathed in yellow light. I barely need it to see my mistake. There is a similarity of style between this brownstone building, at 320 Bainbridge, and the photograph of the synagogue in Boonin's book: tall windows, arched pediments and Palladian lights, center doorway. Mistaken identity: the synagogue in the photograph is three stories and this is two; the synagogue has three windows across and this has five. The synagogue in the photograph may be a superficial copy of the other building, but hadn't I seen? Street to book, book to street, my eyes steel themselves, my neck stiffens.

The caption under the photograph of the synagogue includes the address: 322 Bainbridge.

Then where is it? The apartment house at 322 Bainbridge doesn't say. The windows and floors have been entirely rearranged. Covered in stucco and four stories tall with simple, dignified architectural details, it could be a mausoleum. It's possible that the bones of the synagogue are buried there. The only clue is the dentil work along the cornice; it appears to match the photo.

Sometime in the 1990s our bar closes. I remember now the new name: The Latest Dish. Ravenous suddenly, I go inside Kabobeesh. The décor appears borrowed from a funeral parlor, air conditioning suitable for a corpse or a meat locker. It smells of cardamom. My mother, Hilda, is unfaithful to my father. She has secret trysts in the woods outside our house. Each time she is caught, at first, I side with her. I am eleven. It must be my father's fault. His restaurants fail one after the other; he holds on to pure ideas. I go up to the counter and place my order. I get an assortment of Turkish salads, no meat, and pay the bill. But I leave before the food is ready, and press into the darkness of the alley.

Drunk, we stumble along the wall halfway down this alley outside our bar, late on the desolate night of October 11, 1990, long before the street lamps and trees are installed on South Street. "Now!" I cry out, ecstatic, "Let's go get married."

Eva tears at my shirt with her strong hands; she backs up, backs away, and sprints east down the alley, Kater Street. I don't see her again for three weeks.

18

Wʜᴏ sɪᴛs ᴀʟʟ ᴅᴀʏ in the library's microfilm and newspaper room? Men with beards who years ago might have been agitators or poets, men in white socks, pasty-faced men at microfilm machines intent on obscurity, men without a place to live, men who don't work because of age or infirmity or mental illness, men who emit a terrible dangerous body odor: they read the *Financial Times* and sleep.

I have a favorite machine, to the right of the doorway, facing out. It feels precariously close to the edge. Boxes of microfilm rolls are stacked before me. I scroll through every paper from Yom Kippur 1889. Rewind. The microfilm flaps erratically, like a fish on the end of the line. I try 1888 and 1890 too. There are no newspaper reports of the arrest of the men from Shavel for assaulting the peddler Moscowitz.

For the 1891 incident I have better luck. I learn that the walls of the second-floor hall at 512 S. 3rd Street are filled with red muslin banners with white lettering on Sunday evening, October 11, 1891, Kol Nidre, the start of Yom Kippur. *The World is Our Fatherland. Humanity is Our Family. Socialism is Our Religion.* Other banners are presumably in Yiddish. Sergeant John Wood of the Third District police station has sent a couple of stool pigeons to listen in and report back. They sit with the fifty or so attendees, "Russian Hebrews."

"Socialists Raided," reports the *Inquirer.*

"Who Are These People?" wonders the *North American.*

Things get tense around ten o'clock, or so the officers say. Speechmakers, they say, including Prenner and Gillis (though likely Weinberg), are winding up the crowd, threatening to kill the President, overthrow the government, run the streets with policemen's blood. The *Inquirer* calls Gillis "Maurice"; both papers call Prenner "Brenner." Perhaps this is an alias. Perhaps the room is filled with both socialists and anarchists, as the *North American* says. Anarchists have a collectivist nature. Socialists are free spirited. This can be confusing for anyone.

Wood's squad "swoops in." They arrest Gillis and Prenner. They clean the place out. They remove the Yiddish signs and send them for translation. "A large number of empty beer bottles were found in the place where the raid was made."

The night of speeches on Kol Nidre, the start of Yom Kippur, is to be followed by a parade and picnic along the river in Camden. On Monday, instead of enjoying themselves at a picnic, Prenner and Gillis, who was arrested accidentally instead of Weinberg, are arraigned in front of Magistrate Milligan and held on bail.

Tuesday they stand before Judge Biddle in Quarter Sessions Court No. 2.

Craig Biddle, third son of Nicholas Biddle, born 1823. Nicholas Biddle is president of the Second Bank of the United States, an elitist, polymath, a poet. America under his vision will be the rebirth of Ancient Greece, with a regulated economy, cosmopolitan cities, and free public schools. He is destroyed by Andrew Jackson, in the manner of a schoolyard bully beating up the smartest kid in the class, with the demagogic admiration of every other kid shamed by the smart one's intelligence. A birth of populism. Not long after Nicholas's death as a broken man, Craig's brother Charles becomes a hero in the Mexican War. But Charles becomes a Copperhead in the years to come, a Democrat, a member of the party still in thrall to the myth of his father's enemy, Jackson. Craig Biddle serves in the Civil War, a Republican on the Union side, and takes his place as a marshal in the long procession of Lincoln's remains through the city on April 22, 1865. He rules as a judge in the style of the schoolyard monitor. "Judge Biddle, of Philadelphia, deserves the recognition of the nation for the fearless manner in which he is enforcing the laws in that ring-environed city." A ring is a mob of influence men.

Prenner and Gillis aren't alone in the courtroom in front of Judge Biddle. With them, according to the newspapers and the docket of the Quarter Sessions Court, are Louis Jacobs and Julius Moskowitz.

It's easy to see why the names Louis and Julius are confused.

Though the clerk's handwriting is clear and elegant. The P in Prenner glides up to the J in Jacobs, which loops around the M in Moskowitz. They are like monkeys in a chain.

After his arrest on October 11, the prison warden, Kane, places Moskowitz in the prison entry docket. The clerk spells his name Moskowatz. He is charged with Breach of Peace, Incitement to Riot. According to the arresting officer, Caspar, Julius had not only been distributing fliers advertising the Yom Kippur Ball, but flaunting them "in the faces of the more devout Jews."

Who produces the sensation of flaunting, the flaunter or the flaunted?

The editor-in-chief of the *Public Ledger*, William McKean, writes a letter to Judge Biddle, agreeing with his position and lauding his moral clarity on the subject of personal responsibility. "That whilst a man is sober enough to understand what he is doing, and the consequences of his acts, and to form an intention—he is fully answerable to the law—even though he may have been 'drinking' to the extent ten twenty or thirty drinks." The handwriting is scrawling. We don't imagine Moskowitz being drunk so much as fevered for the cause. Judge Biddle saves this letter; it remains among his personal papers kept at the Pennsylvania Historical Society. The papers fill three boxes, organized in neat files. The letter stretches top to bottom of a modest-sized note page. "Office of the Public Ledger," it says at the top in red, in masthead typeface. The letter appears to be the product of a single thought jotted down—the idea of personal responsibility. It has been folded, stuck in an envelope, probably hand-delivered.

History goes on, without interruption, perhaps without responsibility.

Just one block separates the office of the newspaper and the judge's quarters. I reread the letter, which I have photographed. The editor gives pretense for writing. He is sending along payment for a court fee incurred by his court reporter, unnamed. And while he is at it, a seasoned influence man, he will laud the judge. "It is admirable . . ." One sentence indicates payment, the next ethical accord. Perhaps the specific reference to ten or twenty or thirty drinks points to a particular case—the one the court reporter had been covering. It is also equally plausible that the editor is acknowledging the behavior of the reporter—journalists are condemned to certain tics. Is the fee a penalty assessed by the judge for bad behavior? Or has the editor made a personal reference, a needling? Perhaps it is the judge, known for his sober rulings, who has a penchant for drink? Biddle's father is known to have a terrible habit of hypocrisy, at least that's how the political cartoonists put it. He rarely ceases, they are apt to point out, to undermine his own moral position.

The religious Jews who assault Julius Moskowitz at his peddler's stand in the Washington Market in 1889 and who will seek revenge two years later have been inside the synagogue for hours, since early morning. Their day of fasting and atonement for sin, the purpose of the holiday, has begun the evening before with the communal recitation of a prayer called *Kol Nidre*. The same name is often applied to the entire evening service, and it is this that Moskowitz and his comrades want to subvert with beer and speeches on the night of October 11, 1891.

I've never paid much attention to the prayer until now, searching for the text in English on the Internet. The prayer begs annulment of God's judgment for having broken an oath. "May we be absolved of them, may we be released from them, may they be null and void and of no effect. May they not be binding upon us. Such vows shall not be considered vows; such renunciations, no renunciations; and such oaths, no oaths."

What sort of oath?

"All vows, renunciations, promises, obligations, oaths, taken from this Day of Atonement till the next, may we attain it in peace, we regret them in advance."

They can't be held responsible.

Russian authorities use the language of the prayer to subjugate Jews in the Pale of Settlement. This is proof a Jew can't be trusted. He won't keep his word. For centuries, rabbis attempt to remove the prayer from the liturgy because it confuses the idea of atonement. Then it reappears, like an indelible stain. To defend it, some scholars argue that it concerns oaths to oneself or God only. Others imagine it is merely a practical way to annul vows made under duress or panic. The men of Shavel chant the prayer, which may or may not absolve them of personal responsibility, with the customary haunting melody. The morning after, they recite prayers of reflection on moral failure. They study self-indulgence. They mount toward contrition. In this practice mount the layers of their hearts that Moskowitz is going to tear away.

On Yom Kippur 1889, the morning after the ritual chanting of *Kol Nidre*, the religious wear white to project a feeling of purity. At midday, they stretch their legs and find Moskowitz, also dressed, to the best of a peddler's ability, all in white. The sun—the day is warm, near seventy—catches hold of the white robes, the ritual scarves, the skullcaps. Perhaps the glimmer is blinding. Perhaps the *Kol Nidre* had a subtle effect on the men, who must beg forgiveness and reach out to holiness. *But we may not be able to keep our word. We are only human.* Susceptible to flaunting. Perhaps not responsible.

Yet, according to the Third District officer on duty that day, they are answerable to the law that prohibits the assault of an innocent man.

We might form a picture of a poor peddler standing outside his stand in the ramshackle market. He is a bull, quietly daring. Near to the ground, sensitive to the earthy quality of all life, he can hear, below his own necessarily strident voice, the melody of Hebrew prayer, and he can't deny its beauty. Weinberg implies that Moskowitz is poor, but then what anarchist isn't poor? What Jew isn't a little afraid? A Russian Jew, particularly. The German Jews, even, find him disgusting. The nonreligious Jews find his political views distasteful, worse: a waste of time. Everyone else is apoplectic. All this is arrayed around him like a system of fences. The melody of the Hebrew prayer is probably the largest hole in the fence. At trial two years later, Judge Biddle instructs the court that he isn't deciding guilt or innocence in the case of Moskowitz and the other radicals. He merely must determine if there is enough evidence to substantiate the need for a trial. This is five days after the arrest, October 16, 1891. "Now, decades after it happened, it would still sound to us like a second-rate comedy," writes Weinberg. Why are the four being held? No one is sure, but there are witnesses from the Jewish quarter. Prenner, says one witness, has suggested in a speech that the streets ought to run with capitalist blood (presumably to mix with the blood of policemen). Moskowitz is not only handing out literature, he's assaulting religious Jews. The anarchists see a frame-up orchestrated by a man named Simon Mayer, friend of the cloak manufacturer Blum, whom Prenner and other strikers have almost destroyed during a long labor fight. Mayer has hired the witnesses as a matter of revenge.

How well does Moskowitz speak English? How much can he understand?

Nicholas Biddle is depicted in dozens of political cartoons as the villain at war with Andrew Jackson. Biddle in a toga (he is a renowned Grecophile), Biddle in tall hat, Biddle at the center of the many-headed hydra that is his bank. I search for an image of the judge, his son Craig, a portrait, perhaps, but don't find one. Thomas Sully once paints Craig, at 16, with rosy cheeks (all Sully subjects have rosy cheeks), but the painting has disappeared. What the anarchists have been saying, Judge Biddle counsels the court, is seditious. They are foreigners. They have come to this country voluntarily. No one has forced them to come here! And they attack our institutions. Thus they must be held for trial. "They are enemies to the human race."

19

SOMEHOW I FIND *Repetition* and *Fear and Trembling*, in the single red-and-black Princeton edition, in a box in the basement. I decide to reread *Repetition* as a way to trigger memory of that time at 417 S. 49th Street. I read the opening section, the "Report by Constantin Constantius," a fictional advisor to Kierkegaard's imagined young man, a poet, involved with a young woman, "the beloved." Constantius advises the poet to deceive his beloved so that she will give up on him. "Now I easily grasped the whole situation. The young girl was not his beloved: she was the occasion that awakened the poetic in him and made him a poet." The problem is that the poet, who is in love, has transformed the love into poetic, and therefore false, or abstract, feeling. He can't therefore experience the vital repetition of love, toward faith. A quarter century ago I marked the passage along the margin edge in black pen with a star and an unreadable notation that begins with a clear "E," but may or may not say "Eva." But my eyes glaze, and though it is only eight in the evening and the fan brushes back and forth across my face, I fall asleep. When I stir, I walk up the stairs to the desk on the third floor of my house on Aspen

Street and find a pencil. I underline the passage, my new, hesitant pencil marks carefully approaching the old.

In the "Historical Introduction" to *Repetition* I read—out of necessity to shake myself awake and focus my attention on words and concepts I can comprehend—that, according to Kierkegaard, "an author's private experience can legitimately be used in his writing only in transmuted form, that is, as the universally human, not as personal disclosure." Kierkegaard intends that only a single, "silent" reader should approach his text as personal disclosure, and therefore not universal. This is Regine Olsen, whom he asks to marry in September 1840, the model for the beloved in *Repetition*. The engagement lasts until Kierkegaard breaks it a year later. "My love cannot find expression in a marriage," he writes. "The moment it becomes a matter of actuality, all is lost, then it is too late." Marriage kills the poetic, he thinks. Constantius might say it begins the search for love. On the opposite page, someone, in blue ink, has placed quotes around "Regine." The marks betray the clean, clear handwriting of Eva.

20

THE NEXT MORNING, Nadia and I take a taxi from the office to Bainbridge Street. The streets are nearly empty, as if already the sun has eliminated all life. She tells me about a book she's just read—her father has sent it. The story is about a Beirut architect who spends all his time wandering around the city instead of working. His firm is floundering. Everyone is on edge because of terrorists' bombs, but at the same time real estate developers are manically building, as if cheating death. The architect is missing out on all this business. He does anything to avoid working. He even takes up swimming and cooking. Then he drops dead of a heart attack.

"You read it in Arabic?" I ask.

"Of course," she answers.

The idea of interpretation all of a sudden seems impossible. "I find everything inscrutable," I say, but I don't know if she's listening. The driver, a tall African who hasn't enough legroom, tells us it's time for the United States to elect a female president. "Let the women have a turn," he says. Nadia is listening intently. She pays for the cab with our company credit card. In French, as we leave the cab, she wishes him good luck.

Eva has this same capacity with language. The first time she meets Hilda, my mother, she speaks to her in Dutch. I'm not even aware she knows Dutch. Later, she tells me that, as a teenager, acquiring languages was a way to escape her childhood life. "The colony is a very parochial, provincial, closed-in place," she says; "for all the obeisance to freedom, it's really a kind of prison."

Nadia and I stand in the very place where Reginald's Corolla was parked the night Eva told me Reginald had taken her to the clinic for the abortion. We stand there in the naked heat and blink against the ferocity.

"I don't understand why Americans stand in the full sun," says Nadia. "When it's like this you move to the shade, even the tiniest tree."

All the morning I've been on edge, sweating doubly. I point across the street to the line of trees that replaced the Washington Market. "We have shade!" I try to sound hopeful.

We sit at a bench under a cherry tree at the end of the block, facing west; the parking lot is on the right in front of us, so that we will be able to see it as we talk. Love of Mercy is behind us on the left. I can't take my eyes off it. Nadia notices my uncomfortable wrenching and I try to distract her. "Listen: there is hardly a single bird up there in the tree."

"See. It's even too hot for them."

"Even in the shade . . . The asphalt buckles . . ."

"What do you keep looking at?"

"Nothing—nothing. Let's talk about the Terzian building."

"I'm done talking about it." She pulls her sunglasses over her eyes. "Is someone you know over there?" she wonders.

"Someone?"

"OK, so who is Moscowitz?"

"What? What do you mean?"

"I don't mean you. Nicholas. But you know what I'm talking about. I've seen the papers on your desk. You're doing family research?"

"—"

"All your time on the Internet. At the library? Is that where you go?"

"Just old ghosts."

"No."

"I went in search of answers, Nadia, and it opened up all kinds of questions. I went to find out more about this neighborhood, to really understand it, because I'm searching for a new approach to the work, or the old way has gotten stale. I'm sorry."

"You're supposed to be designing this building, finding more commissions. Why are you even paying me?"

"There's a bird in the tree, I hear it—a single, courageous bird."

"You're prepared to lose this commission? We're going to. You know you've stopped giving me direction—you've stopped even thinking about this project. I assume there aren't any others?"

"A few phone calls, an RFP . . . but it has passed." My voice is a near whisper. After some silence I add: "I am thinking about it." My voice drops out again on "thinking."

"You know this now, but I have to leave . . . ," she starts to say. "I was trained to find the right solution, to search and search for the right solution. I don't think you understand about the education system in other places, somewhere like where I am from—you're never allowed to stop seeking the truth, the right answer. It's about strength of mind."

"Tenacity maybe."

"Tenacity maybe." And then, "But then I try to understand. Are you going to let this go—this great site, this beautiful neighborhood? That is foolish."

"No—no, let's get back to work, let's . . . let's keep seeking answers. It's not time yet."

"It is. I'm sorry—it is. I'm going to Paris and when I return . . ." I wrench again to lay eyes on Love of Mercy, if that is even it. I don't hear the rest.

Nadia is standing under the tree looking at her phone.

I beg her to reconsider. I promise a raise. I offer more responsibility. "Go to Paris when this is over."

"But then what comes next?"

Pressed in under a low branch of the cherry tree, I stick my hand into the thick of the leaves; Terzian's offer plays over in my head. The bark is smooth and rough equally. The leaves are hot purple-green and cupping. But it is cooler here, and Nadia, lighting a cigarette, relents.

"For now . . ."

Guilt invades the gratitude, then unease follows, sharp and heavy and blunt, shame for leading her this way.

But Nadia doesn't feel shame. She just presses forward. And I've avoided her questions about Moskowitz. They will come again, perhaps right away, but just then the poet Popkin passes by. He seems deep in thought and untouched by the heat. I let him go without saying anything. A few seconds later, I change my mind. I call out his name. Popkin is confused. He often seems this way, as if he's carrying on multiple conversations at once. He can't keep track. I ask if he still leaves poems anonymously. "Oh, they aren't anonymous," he says. "My name is on them. Maybe you mean the reader is anonymous to me—the silent reader."

Then it occurs to me that Popkin may not keep even a second copy of each poem. This seems to me absurdly romantic. I begin to ask if this is so when Nadia reaches out her hand to shake his. I make the official introduction. She explains that he's in the Street View photograph of the parking lot we're going to replace with a building. The poet hasn't seen the Street View image, but he isn't surprised. "It's no coincidence," he says, eyes wide. He walks this way for coffee in the afternoon. "Actually, if you want to know the truth," he says, "I do often stare into that parking lot and dream of something else."

21

ON OCTOBER 16, the day Prenner, Gillis, Jacobs, and Moskowitz appear before Judge Biddle, the clerk enters his name in the court docket, "Julius Moskowitz." The clerk has placed a check next to the name of each defendant. He notes the men were kept at County Prison, a crenelated fortress just south of the Jewish quarter. After the hearing, another clerk, writing in a coarse and dark hand, notes, "Loui Jacobs and Julius Moskowitz remanded." Fingerprints in red-brown smudge, a result of the deteriorating leather binding, crowd the edge of the page, like the muddy water of a receded flood. The clerk has added an additional hash mark next to Moskowitz's name. Is this to say he appears doubly guilty? But on further inspection, the extra line is the cross of the t in Moskowitz. The line has gone astray.

"I'm no longer seeking answers," I say in a whisper. No one in the archives seems to hear. Am I talking to Nadia or Eva?

Moskowitz, do you feel like you're wrongly accused?

Brother, are you scared? Did Biddle frighten? Does Judge Arnold intimidate?

Can you follow the court proceedings?

Do you feel an urge to tear the courtroom down?

Have you noticed the great girth of the prison?

Friday, January 8, 1892. The case of Moskowitz is the fifth of the day in the courtroom of Judge Michael Arnold. October to January, Moskowitz is in County Prison for almost three months. County Prison is also called Moyamensing Prison. You can find an 1838 engraving of the prison on the Internet. The engraving is by the artist J. C. Wild, from his book *Panorama and Views of Philadelphia and Its Vicinity*. Thomas Ustick Walter, who will build the new addition to the U.S. Capitol in Washington, D.C., designs the prison with gothic turrets and battlements, a castle of the dispossessed. Walter, who is of Scottish descent, must be drawing on a memory. Two horses pull a carriage down the Passyunk Road (as it is called then); two boys play along the wall of the stone fortress. The enormous prison dominates the landscape that defines their world. Yet the skill of the architect renders it human to the passersby. It must be imprinted on the memory of thousands of neighbors, still. Wild, the artist, bathes the prison in southern light and one of the boys casts a shadow along the base of the wall. The shadow takes the shape of a rattlesnake half upright, as if on alert.

The prison is a flight of visual fancy. The Temple of Amenhotep III, on the Nile, inspires Walter's design of the debtors' section. What possesses the architect's mind? Amenhotep III is the artist of the desert. He dresses Egypt in statuary. He delights in the colossal. Even in the land of the pyramids, his mortuary temple explodes the imagination. Floods gnaw at it for two hundred years, leaving it in ruins. Walter takes a nibble for Philadelphia. Is this an act of resurrection? I look again at the engraving by J. C. Wild. How romantic County Prison appears on my computer screen! A gentle breeze, a fair day. A building emits conflicting gestures.

Moskowitz won't be held in the Egyptian wing. By 1891, that part of the prison is used for women. Kate Matters is arraigned the day after Julius, for "Assault & Abuse." She is locked up in Amenhotep's trace. Moskowitz is placed, awaiting trial, in a nine by eleven cell with an arched ceiling. Julius is defendant number 492. Fifth case, "Commonwealth versus Julius Muscowetz."

22

Perhaps architecture is a game of scale. Amenhotep III carves himself into giant sculptures that guard his temple. The architect Walter reduces it to a quarter city block so that, walking by, you might be reminded of great worlds far beyond. In the same way, I imagine, a courtroom boils things down—as if a stage—so that true emotion might be amplified. What happens in the process—going upscale and then downscale—is distortion.

The air in Judge Arnold's courtroom is xenophobic. The four defendants are foreigners. Are they socialists or anarchists? Are they Single Taxers? It doesn't matter. They simmer in the same pot. Quarter Sessions Court No. 2 flanks Independence Hall on the right. It suffers no traitors. It will defend its freedoms.

The costume department has been busy. Hair and makeup on call!

> **Prosecutor** (unnamed in the records): Who is he? Where was he born? He comes from Siberia? Answer me, do you or do you not believe in God?

Witness [a Mr. Forvein, "exactly as our enemies imagine a typical revolutionary," says Weinberg, "with long hair and shabby clothes"]: No.
Prosecutor: That is enough for me.

Weinberg scribbles notes. Natasha Notkin, twenty-one years old, a nihilist and freethinker, is the next witness for the defense. One hundred twenty-two years later it is still possible to fall in love with Natasha.

Prosecutor: Where are you from?
Witness [Notkin]: From Russia.
Prosecutor: When did you cut off your hair?
Witness: In Russia.
Prosecutor: Are you a Nihilist?
Witness: I don't know what that is.

What stories does a building tell? Which things are remembered? Which things are washed away?

A few feet from where Julius Muscowetz sits, on the bench assigned to defendants, a mob of grimy radicals storms into an English Royal courtroom. It is 1776. Like savages they tear down the coat of arms and haul out the portrait of the king. The flames that form in burning these items draw backwards across the Atlantic Ocean and ignite at the Bastille. Can one think about the American Revolution without thinking about the French, or vice versa?

Perhaps it is our peculiar nature, as a people, to see our own revolution as exceptional, as disconnected, as stand-alone.

"What the accused want here in this country is a French Revolution!" says the prosecutor, unaware of the concept of irony. "Find them guilty—stop their devilish plans."

Julius, do you sit forward? A Jew from the Pale of Settlement understands bitter irony, is vulnerable to arbitrary declaration. Do you remain impassive? Do you laugh—even inside your muscular frame—do you say to yourself, "A second-rate Russian prefect wouldn't . . ."?

Reading Weinberg's account of the trial over and over, I look for even the slightest indication, a subtle turn of phrase, a hidden reference. Moskowitz starts the trial and now Muscowetz will end it. Are you a new man? How dare you come to this country, digest its freedom, and stab it in the back? How dare you? Do you feel shame now, Julius? Or do you insist you are still right? Do you shout, instead, "What's the use of freedom? What's it for?"

How dare you, Julius? Oh, but you are a good man, a moral man, aren't you? Isn't this why you've joined the movement? To help people, to seek justice for everyone, your wish isn't to fight. And precisely because you are moral, and Julius, precisely because you adore people, Julius, shame finds you, for what Boonin calls "tearing out the heart" of the religious Jews. Shame procures tears from your eyes.

The prosecutor is blinded by his bit of theater. He doesn't look at the apostates. He turns to the jury instead. "Show thus your true patriotism for the fatherland in a critical time. This decisive moment stands before us all now as never before in the whole history of America."

Boil down, and blow up.

The prosecutor is an architect erecting a tabernacle of justice. He draws a line. He digs a foundation. He buries pylons. He puts up a wall. The prosecutor's wall is meant to divide people. Patriots from foreigners, the shameful from the shameless, for this is the "decisive moment."

Cohen says that in 1889, standing outside the synagogue at his peddler stand, Moskowitz (for that is how the name is spelled in my translation) reads a "pure prayer." But what is that prayer? Earlier, I have speculated that the pure prayer is a manifesto of Johann Most. That year, while living in New York (and frequenting Philadelphia), Most publishes an appeal, "Anarchist Communism." True communists are anarchists and true anarchists are communists, he implores, and for both to achieve their ends the present government must be destroyed and all property put in common. "They make revolutionary propaganda because they know the privileged class can never be overturned peacefully." The propaganda Most has in mind is what he calls "propaganda of the deed": violent action. He is often thrown in jail.

Architecture is often violent like this, always tearing down, building over, covering up, canceling out. But what would it mean to really tear down, to build justly? Terzian wouldn't be pleased to know.

In March 1892, near the end of the trial of Prenner, Gillis, Jacobs, and Muscowetz, police raid a hotel in Paris, on rue de l'Arbre Sec, a block from the Louvre. The story is reported in the *Philadelphia Inquirer*. They arrest 60 anarchists and seize what they say are chemicals used to make explosives: chlorate of potassium and hydrochloric acid.

Could these be the chemicals used to bomb French military barracks nearby a few days before? The bombing injures none of the 800 guards who live at the barracks. The barracks themselves are heavily damaged, though. The stained glass of the church of St. Gervais, from the sixteenth century, is "ground to atoms." Two men, identified in the press as "Companions X and Z," release a statement: "Yes, it is by terror that we will overcome the present state of things."

A few days earlier, in Washington, D.C., the United States Congress authorizes a new federal immigration office to regulate the flood of incoming aliens (I read about this in the *Inquirer*, too, on microfilm through the amber cloud of the old screen). The following kinds of people are excluded from admission, above and beyond earlier laws:

Idiots
Insane persons
Paupers or persons likely to become a public charge

Persons suffering from a loathsome or dangerous conta-
gious disease

Persons who have been convicted of a felony or other
infamous crime or misdemeanor involving moral
turpitude

Polygamists

Any person whose ticket or passage is paid for with the
money of another

Anarchists aren't singled out—there is no ideological lit-
mus test in the law, and won't be for another dozen years, until
after the assassination of William McKinley by Leon Czol-
gosz. The real "critical moment," then, the political opportunity to plug the hole in the wall, has dangerously passed.
Thus the prosecutor's heightened rhetoric, the prayer of des-
peration. If the U.S. Congress won't act, you in the jury box,
you had better.

23

BOARDING THE NUMBER thirty-four trolley, do I feel a bit like
Constantin Constantius? Kierkegaard's narrator couldn't exactly be trusted, especially since everyone knew he was in-
vented, a figment of the philosopher's imagination. Ah, but
I am on a mission to understand my own young love. The
number thirty-four trolley rides up Baltimore Avenue. I step
down at 49th Street. For safety reasons, back then, Eva gets
off at 48th Street. The worry is the New World Lounge on
the corner of 49th, where immigrant men stand on the sidewalk day and night leering. The triangle-shaped park that
comes to its point just in front of the lounge is worn thin by
time and disinvestment. The triangle is called Cedar Park,
which is also the name of the neighborhood where we live.
At the wide end of the park is the church led by a giant man,
Reverend Patterson, who wears on his ring, which is the size
of a rose blossom, an eagle and a snake. East of the church,
in an ornate Renaissance Revival firehouse built in 1903 and
turned into a farmers' market in 1988, a butcher named Leon-
ard Brown sells goat and lamb. Harris, our housemate, says
that once you begin eating meat this good nothing else will

do. Mr. Brown's meat is our indulgence. Only Abigail, a vegetarian, doesn't profit.

The neighborhood, far west of our university, might be a world apart. Living here makes us feel authentic and original, as if we, who are merely transient, are part of something real.

Stepping off the trolley, I recall the presence of anarchists here in the neighborhood. In the twentieth century, anarchists moved across the southern vector of the city, across the Schuylkill River and into this neighborhood with its reserved Victorian airs, its turrets, porticos, and gabled roofs. I step into Moskowitz's legacy, and I have been here before. For a few intense days in late winter and spring 1990, when, after the abortion, the relationship between Eva and me had become erratic and exhausting, I followed Reginald into the anarchist houses along Baltimore Avenue, where he spent his free time. The houses are still, today, in poor repair. Several have hand-painted anarchist signs hung across the columns of the porches. Though I want to see our house a few blocks north, at 417 S. 49th Street, I detour for a moment back into this erratic world.

In the days after the oil refinery protest, I despaired of half attempts to organize on campus; no one really seemed to care. Clubs formed, or others expanded, but only to put on an Earth Day celebration. On an unexpectedly warm day, I recall putting up posters for an upcoming rally. The tape snapped like a magnet. My fingers got caught up. My scalp bristled. I sensed my own half commitment. I joined a protest march to City Hall. Probably a few dozen others had also joined. Many were overweight, their beards gray. The chant was melodic, holy. I forgot for a moment where I was and I nearly ran into someone, a laborer or a mechanic, possibly, with grease stains on his hands and shirt. I tried to apologize. I hadn't seen him. We're marching peacefully, I said, scrambling for words, to raise awareness about pollution. We shouldn't be cowed by big business. The words slid across my tongue. He undid me with his stare. He saw through me.

I recall following my dissatisfaction into the anarchist houses along Baltimore Avenue. The days that followed the protest—ten or fifteen days in March 1990 when classes were out because of spring break—were a viscous web of sleeplessness and music, drugs and sex, and cats everywhere—on wooden floors, on bare carpets. No one there cared about a half-hearted protest against pollution, unless the point was to tear down the entire military-industrial complex.

I remember now falling in with a friend of Reginald, an eighteen-year-old named Genevieve from Detroit. She wears black, like everyone, and works, when she can, as a messenger. Genevieve is kind, but she doesn't laugh easily. She likes me, but she doesn't trust men and in bed she prefers women. The main idea, anyway, is personal freedom: I claim mine, you claim yours, and we respect each other's. The police are paid to disrespect our personal freedom. The police are agents of the state. We talk obsessively about this.

One day, it is cold again, and Genevieve has a job to transport some boxes from one office to another. She asks me to help her. We take the trolley to City Hall and then transfer to the Frankford Elevated, north. We get off at York-Dauphin and head east into a district filled with old textile mills, offices, and dye houses, a part of Kensington. Snow pegs our faces and everything is gray—even red brick and terracotta. We are to box up the offices of a textile company, which once made sweaters and has gone into receivership, and transport the boxes to the bank that now owns the assets. Why Genevieve has been hired to do this isn't clear. I ask, but I can't make sense of her answer. A man greets us outside a steel door. He unlocks the door without further words. Then, when we're inside, he cautions there may be junkies there. "Let's hope they haven't set any fires," he mumbles. Genevieve is shy; she manages a slight smile and then shrugs. The man gives us the key and leaves.

Genevieve lights a cigarette. She offers me my own, but I decline, listening for voices or movement. Is anyone inside? She kids that I am straight, but corrects herself and says I am "sweet." She is a tender thing, in truth, and I wonder if she has had a decent life. Files, receipts, carbon copies of letters, material samples, accounting ledgers, these are all over the floor, which is also filled with dust, pigeon scat, mouse droppings, paint chips, and Styrofoam cups. She sits in a windowsill. I start to stack papers. I stop and wander around the office; I find where the junkies have set a fire—in a room full of Jacquard looms. The floor is charred, but it doesn't seem as if anyone has been here recently. Following the looms through a massive loft I find myself in an older section of the mill; I gaze through a window at the stone courtyard and the slender chimney. Looking out, a mysterious yearning for buildings takes hold of me; in this moment I must have decided to become an architect.

When I return, Genevieve is hoisting boxes; she has apparently gotten to work. Moving to help, I realize she is taking things out of boxes—sweaters, each individually wrapped in plastic, army issue. "Made in the U.S.A.," she says.

For a while I don't really understand what she's doing and I return to making piles.

"What are you doing?" she says.

"What do you mean, 'what am I doing?'"

Pale skin, short hair, her gaze lands on me. "Come over here and help me get these sweaters in these two boxes and let's get out of here."

She means to take the sweaters to Baltimore Avenue—"It's cold out still, if you haven't noticed." And the job? She doesn't answer.

I protest.

She says she has no idea what I'm saying. "Go, if you want."

"It makes sense, what you want to do—"

"Go, if you want," she repeats, and nods.

But I don't go. I help Genevieve clean out the army surplus sweaters that have never made it to the loading dock, thousands of dollars' worth of sweaters.

What am I doing fumbling about these tumbledown memories? Avoiding my office, Nadia, the Terzian commission. Searching for traces of Eva or Julius, it can only be, and stumbling back on myself.

Now I drift farther down Baltimore Avenue, porch after porch, each house a twin, or a pair, a house that could only exist with another, identical house. That time long ago, I carry a box and Genevieve carries the other and by the time we climb the stairs to the porch our fingers sting from the cold, our arms shake uncontrollably. She hugs me and without thinking one way or the other, I let her go inside, alone. I sit on the porch rail and then a half hour later, still there, I walk out to the avenue and turn right at 49th Street and go home. In the days that follow, for the time being, until our passion boils over again, Eva and I will reconcile.

It isn't hard to follow these same steps, today; now, as then, I feel my pace quicken and the blocks of apartment houses beyond the New World Lounge, painted cream now and almost elegant, breeze by. After Hazel Avenue, the Tudor style becomes predominant, and this is how I know, even after all these years, I am nearing home. 417 S. 49th Street is an easy house for the five of us, Eva and I and Reginald, Harris, and Abigail. It is easy, I should say, until it isn't.

There is a tiny lawn in front of the house, guarded by a wall of ivy. The grass is meager in March, but at the edge, orange and purple crocuses are cutting through. In late afternoon on a summer day, as it is now, I stand with my back to the house and lean against the wall of ivy. The sun cuts across the top of my head and I recall the sound of Eva's voice and then Reginald's, Harris's, and Abigail's, like the ancient sound one discovers in the quiet of a forest, a specter of sounds that have been there all along. I turn from the sun and notice that the original English windows have survived. I can't help but notice, too, a For Sale sign in the center of the tiny lawn.

NATHANIEL POPKIN

24

Eva runs east down Kater Street, on October 11, 1990, after I propose marriage, exactly ninety-nine years after Julius Moskowitz is arrested on the same block at 512 S. 3rd Street. Despite my proposal, I don't think much of her escape. She has raised herself; her sense of responsibility contains also its opposite, an unfurling, a letting go. I must let her go.

The next night, while I am at home at 417 S. 49th Street, she calls. "Don't go to the police," she says in a rushed voice. She hangs up.

I wonder, will she be in class? The next book we are to read is *The Concept of Anxiety*.

Abigail is Eva's oldest friend, from the summer camp she was allowed to attend in the San Juan Islands at age eleven. Abigail says she will find her. In my modesty of emotion I don't realize that I am being too cool, too calm. Eva needs something and I'm not listening.

Having left Nadia in the office, I unstack the striking Princeton editions of Kierkegaard's works and arrange them on my desk on the third floor. Inside the front cover of *The Concept of Anxiety*, I notice now, Reginald has drawn pictures, in an effort to cheer me up: Kierkegaard's bust amended with torso, arms, legs, and shoes; a "double hair whammy," known beyond 417 S. 49th Street as the pudendum; a dog named Spot who is a "physician"; and a hamburger. I have written, in blue ink, on the title page, "No empirical basis for existence of hereditary sin." I have underlined "empirical" and crossed out "hereditary."

Should I call her parents? I ask Abigail. No, she's safe (and they may not even have a phone); Eva has let us know she is safe precisely so we won't try to contact her parents.

Another week goes by. Our professor, Bill Wright, asks me to stay behind after class. Bill is a Californian, blond, tall, handsome, gravelly voice, an unlikely professor of religion, perhaps.

Begging forgiveness, hoping to preempt a scolding, I apologize for dozing during class. Since October 11, I have hardly slept.

"She's OK," says Dr. Wright.

I stutter in response and repeat my apology.

Wright is fatherly but also kind, as if he'd really like to be my friend. "No, you're not listening. Eva, she is your girlfriend, right? She's met with me. She needed some time off."

"She's studying still?" I attempt a calm tone. This is all I can manage.

He assures me that despite missing class Eva is still excelling in her study of Kierkegaard.

"Her books are just inside our house. I could bring them—"

Dr. Wright blinks, almost spasmodically. This is his only detracting feature. I decide I must trust him; he can bring Eva home. As I come to realize this, somehow I also acknowledge that for some reason she won't ever be the same.

25

IT IS SNOWING. Flakes pour from the sky, as if in a hurry. In late winter, they are large, like overripe fruit. They swallow the horse carts and the pressmen.

The courthouse is behind Independence Hall. The courthouse doesn't exist now. The courtroom where Julius sits has large windows. On a normal day, they frame the clock tower of Independence Hall.

No one wants the French Revolution. No one wants the disorder. No one has the right to come here and attack our way of life. The city is chaotic enough. The sidewalks are too narrow. Banks press in on Independence Hall. Insurance, real estate, finance. Newspaper offices crowd the corner. I count seven of them on the 1895 map. The *Public Ledger*'s building is closest and most remarkable. By then it has blossomed to six stories, encased in a nest of cast iron with lacy wrought ironwork along the roofline. The cast iron is painted white. It is a clever composition: the weight of the fifth estate, the buoyancy of the truth. Across the middle band of the east façade, overlooking the criminal court, there are ninety-six windows (I count them in a vintage photograph on the computer screen with the tip of a pencil), a palace of glass. March 18, the snow shuffles across the windows as if from the confectioner's can. But not only snow. Steam and smoke, condensation, the white breath of work horses envelop the glass palace, shroud it, swirling and billowing like the ruffled skirt of a mesmerizing dancer. Cast iron is subsumed by the snow and smoke, as it will be by history. I say history not in some vague gesture but because the loss of the building in 1920 is an act of history, an act itself subsumed by the construction of its replacement, a button-down hulk of the colonial revival. That building, which stands today, is a negation.

Trace a U from the Public Ledger Building across 6th Street, down Chestnut Street, across 5th to the other side of Independence Hall. Each of these buildings is gone.

The snow is letting up. But the wind hasn't settled.

In Paris, March 18, police continue a sweep of anarchists' apartments. Four men are suspected of the setting of bombs across the city. They can't be acting alone. A fifth man may be their commander, but no one is sure who he is. Are these men plotting to assassinate the Czar? The best detectives are on the case.

Are you aware, Moskowitz, of the French fighters X and Z? Have you heard about the barracks attack? Do you envision revolution? Or do you act from conscience? From memory? From pain? From fear?

It is the twenty-first anniversary of the Paris Commune. "A quietness that was surprising to the police" settles on the city.

Do the newspapers reach you in the courthouse?

Pressmen stretch their legs inside the courtroom. The floor is wet from snow. Reporters from the *Inquirer*, *North American*, *The Evening Bulletin*, and *The Public Ledger* jam the press box. It is likely there are others, but these are the papers I've been reading on microfilm. The library is best in the early morning. The staff in the newspaper department discusses pensions. A grade-three employment opening has been announced. Someone has been injured on the job.

The prosecutor brings a boy named Michael Vonitzky to the stand. He has heard "blood-thirsty" speeches in the hall at 512 S. 3rd on October 11. Joseph Kramer testifies he's seen Vonitzky point out Morris Gillis to the police. Perhaps it is the boy Vonitzky who has mistaken Gillis for Weinberg.

Gillis, with his limp, is the only defendant to testify. Prenner, Jacobs, and Moskowitz remain seated. "The other defendants were not called by their counsel, who explained to the court that they did not believe in God nor in a state of future rewards and punishments."

But later, Moskowitz, as head of the holy burial society, what will you come to believe then?

The defense calls an immigrant, Adolph Waechter, to testify. He is born in 1864, the same year as Julius. Waechter is a barman. Moskowitz has given up his peddler stand in the Washington Market on Bainbridge Street. Now he runs a newsstand. Waechter lives above it; he's known Julius for six or seven months. He complains to Moskowitz about the pamphlets promoting the Yom Kippur Ball. Perhaps he scorns radical politics—all radicalism ends in tyranny. Moskowitz, according to Waechter, responds with assault.

Waechter's testimony contradicts a statement Moskowitz has given police. (I wonder: does he give the statement under oath?) Julius says he doesn't know Waechter; he's never seen him a day in his life. Another witness, Brussack, says he and Moskowitz work every Saturday together at 2nd and Market. Waechter is mistaken.

Policeman McFarland comes to testify. He says Brussack is wrong. Moskowitz works at the newsstand every Saturday. Is the barman Waechter in cahoots with the police?

The newsstand tantalizes. Nadia is calling me, but I'm in the library. I can't pick up. The gray light is soothing. The white paint of the plaster ceiling is peeling. Flakes are suspended twenty-five feet in the air. Newsstands attract radicals, at least according to Boonin. But where is this one? I try in vain to determine Waechter's address.

Policeman McFarland is the last witness. Julius isn't allowed to testify. He doesn't believe in God and thus can't swear on the bible. What he says can't be trusted. I want to hear his voice. I lean into the microfilm machine. Julius? Aren't you burning up, unable to tell your story?

My phone lights up, Nadia calling again. I hesitate over the slide bar. I let it ring. I put it down. Vibrating, it falls to the floor.

When McFarland sits, the prosecutor stands. Here he delivers the speech I've already mentioned. I wonder if he's conflating the French Revolution with the Paris Commune, celebrating its anniversary that day. Perhaps Weinberg has remembered it wrong. Distant history seems to weigh more, but it's harder to reconstruct.

The judge instructs the jury. Prenner, Gillis, Jacobs, and Moskowitz have been charged with conspiracy, riot, and blasphemy. How will you know if they are guilty? Have these men organized to discuss politics and religion? Or to induce others to violence? Do they seek to overthrow the government? Are they thirsty for blood?

The courthouse behind Independence Hall first appears in the city atlas in 1875. It's called the "New Court House." In 1895 it is called the "Court House." In 1910, the next atlas available on the Internet, it is gone. The court records, too. An archivist explains that only the records of major trials were preserved. She shows me the files for the trial of serial murderer H. H. Holmes, in this same courtroom, in 1895. It is Judge Arnold who sentences Holmes to death.

Novelists and filmmakers, she says, often use the file on Holmes.

I gaze into the box, but the entire year 1892 is missing.

The *New York Times* quotes Judge Arnold at length in the

case of H. H. Holmes. "Flight is the act of a guilty man, and not the act of a cunning man," says the judge before confirming the jury's ruling of guilty.

The final charge in the case of Prenner, Gillis, Jacobs, and Moskowitz is blasphemy. The *Inquirer* and the *Public Ledger* reproduce the words of Judge Arnold directly, without quotation marks but without paraphrasing either: the wording is the same in each paper. Judge Arnold comes off as reflective and sober. In preparing the jury to consider if the accused are guilty of blasphemy, he tells the jury, "Men who do not conscientiously believe in God have a right to say so, but they have no right to blaspheme and thereby hurt the feelings of those people who do believe in a Supreme Being."

I step into the hallway and call Nadia back. "Where are you?" she asks.

I decide to tell the truth: "At the library."

"The library?" She is incredulous. I might have said I was in Beirut. Silence invades the phone connection, presses into my ear, the tip of a weapon.

I sigh.

Something inside of her turns. I can feel this through the silence. Silence guards against humiliation. Then it becomes humiliation. I am experienced with silence.

"You can keep paying me, but I'm through with the Terzian project."

"We discussed this. I thought we discussed this."

"No, no. If you want to prepare what he needs for the neighborhood meeting, go ahead. You can fire me, you can pay me, whatever. But you work it out. My God, Nicholas, who is Julius Moskowitz?"

She hangs up.

Back inside the reading room my research jumbles. I read one thing, put it down, and then remember something else. I need to get it right, as my father needs to get his lamb right. Neither the research nor the lamb really matters. This occurs to me with the force of a sudden wind that sucks a door open and slams it closed.

I pack up the books and my computer and walk out of the library, past the fountain in Logan Square and through a dark cavern of office towers to the underground trolley station, and I wait on the filthy platform for the trolley to West Philadelphia. Water drips down the walls as if this is the inside of a cave. More and more I find myself on this platform, then climbing onto the trolley and, like today, alighting from the back door in late afternoon with the sun in my eyes, like a ghost of myself. I stare at the apartment house on the corner of 49th Street where the trolley halts, with its Victorian massing like a cruise ship, painted red, yellow, and white. A man with purple-brown skin sits on a yellow lawn chair facing south. He makes no expression as I pass on my way to 417 S. 49th Street, as if he hasn't even felt my shadow.

26

THE *EVENING BULLETIN*, at least, has given me the name of the witness Adolph Waechter, born in Switzerland. When I think about the courtroom, Judge Arnold, the prosecutor, our four defendants, Weinberg, and the reporters, my mind often drifts to Waechter, and I wonder if he made a deal with the police. In those days, a barman kicks back profits to the ward boss. The ward boss controls the police precinct. Waechter is a stooge. His testimony, a payback for profits and votes, will send another immigrant to prison.

I think about the courtroom, filled with foreign accents. I think about the sound of those accents, like water boiling that someone has forgotten, and the sound of Judge Arnold's gavel. His gavel makes the sound of colonial revival architecture. That is, negation, but also reclamation. Quiet your foreign voices.

Waechter is large. He wears a cap. He rolls his sleeves, even during a snowstorm. He arrives in the United States in 1879 or 1880, according to census records, and he marries a Philadelphia girl of German descent, Katherine Lauer, who goes by Katie. They have no children. By the time of the trial, Waechter has been in America for a dozen years; tending bar, he's learned to speak in rapid-fire English. Even if many of his customers are themselves immigrants, the English of a barman multiplies; he is accumulating everyone else's test phrases. Alcohol liquefies the process. In the courtroom, however, he will stumble nervously despite the rolled sleeves, the dead strong expression. The German will leak out.

Moskowitz: burly, dark, itinerant. He arrives in 1886 or 1888. The records are inconsistent, probably because he doesn't speak or understand English very well. Possibly because memory has the soul of a liar.

Which of these men will the jury believe? How can they trust you, Julius, if you never speak?

Waechter, born in 1864, is about to celebrate his thirty-eighth birthday. From records taken during the census in 1900, 1920, and 1930, we know Moskowitz is born that same year, but there is no birthdate on his death certificate. According to record #46314, Julius dies at 10:39 p.m. on May 17, 1936, of advanced arteriosclerotic cardiovascular disease. Adolph Waechter (record #112302) dies at 2:28 p.m. on December 14, 1937, of cirrhosis of the liver "with acute hypertension evidenced." The Internet produces this information. "Write plainly in unfading ink—this is a permanent record." These instructions are capitalized along the margin edge of the Pennsylvania certificate of death.

Codes, in the same hand, in what appears to be colored pencil but may be faded ink, are written on both men's death certificates: 124b, 95b (Waechter), 134, 95b (Moskowitz). The handwriting is perfect standard grammar school cursive, as if written by a teacher in chalk. It takes ten minutes searching the Internet to interpret the code, "International List of Causes of Death Revision 4 (1929)." Code 124 signifies cirrhosis. 124b, written on Waechter's death certificate: Cirrhosis of the liver not returned as alcoholic.

Code 134 is kidney disease. A doctor has noted "Vesical calculi: uremia" on Moskowitz's death certificate as a contributing factor in death.

Code 95b, a cause of death shared by these two immigrant men born in 1864, includes two subcategories: (1) Dilation of heart (cause unspecified) and (2) Heart disease (undefined). Is 95b an error in Moskowitz's case? Code 97 would be the proper one for arteriosclerosis.

For two months, Dr. Hartman, of Pine Street, has been treating Waechter, probably at his house in North Philadelphia. Date of onset? asks the form. Dr. Hartman writes, "3 mos? yrs?"

Drs. Muschat and Cantor, of Mt. Sinai Hospital, have been treating Moskowitz since he was brought in on May 15. They operated the next day.

"The atmosphere in the courtroom was charged with hatred toward the 'foreigners,'" writes Weinberg: all the foreigners perhaps but Waechter, who is under the protection of the police.

The jury returns in half an hour. Weinberg never doubts the result. He writes with the intensity of a man under heel: The jury "understood the danger to the fatherland and did their duty: they helped to complete the frame-up of the accused."

"The 'Anarchists' Convicted," reads the *Inquirer*'s headline on Saturday morning. Bail, explains Judge Arnold, can't be extended to them. This isn't a one-time violation; their blasphemy is habitual. "These people must be taught that they must obey the law."

27

THE JURY IN THE TRIAL of Prenner, Gillis, Jacobs, and Moskowitz sentences the radicals to one year in prison. The sentence is dropped to eight months after lobbying by capitalists. They are afraid to foment more anarchist anger. They want Prenner, particularly, on their side. He is smart, ambitious, useful. Come to your senses, Prenner!

Prenner, preening, sees a chance to advance himself. Moskowitz takes notice that some use the movement to consolidate power.

Anarchists collect funds to support the families of the four men. They send Moskowitz's wife four dollars a week. They send the money to Minnie. I try to envision Julius and Minnie. I want to piece together their life together. I want to build the structure of their lives so that I can enter in.

"Who is this Julius Moskowitz?" Nadia, her hair wrapped in a dark cherry-colored scarf, stares at me through my office door. "A relative of yours? You never answer."

"I'm not sure yet." I try to be honest.

"You're still avoiding the question."

"He tried to tear things down . . . and then, I think, he figured out how to build them up."

"A mystic? You're describing a mystic. You sound like my grandmother, Malakeh. She was always telling—no, never mind. Here are the last five phone messages from Terzian's secretary."

"I'm describing an architect, Nadia."

"Julius Moskowitz was an architect?"

"I think so."

"A person who uses her training and skill to solve real problems and create beauty?" She stands over my desk. She deserves answers. How can I give her answers?

"I don't think he had much education," I offer.

"That's it, I want you to know. I'm not taking any more phone messages. I'm not your secretary. You can answer the phone."

She's gone before I can answer.

Julius and Minnie are separated now, he in prison and she at home, waiting, surviving on charity. The Internet doesn't tell me Minnie's political philosophy. On the Yom Kippur morning, 1889, does she dress him in pure white? Or do they argue for hours the night before, disturbing the children? Does she implore, "Don't abandon me for the movement!" I've learned they have at least one child, Harry, listed as "informant" on Julius's death certificate. Does she say, finally, "Go, if you're going, but go with God?"

In the search box I type "1890 U.S. census." The census that year is the first to use punch cards and automated tabulation. It takes only six weeks to calculate the national population of almost sixty-three million. *Scientific American* magazine publishes a lithograph showing operators feeding punch cards into the "electrical counting machines." They are modern, fashionable women. The operator in the foreground wears her hair in a bun. She is intent on her work, calm but happy. A stern man with a handlebar mustache supervises; perhaps the operator smiles for his benefit. Minnie, I surmise, and the census operators, are about the same age as Nadia. Minnie's husband is part of a movement with modern, radical women. But for some reason I don't imagine her this way.

In 1921, about a quarter of the 1890 census records burn in a fire in the U.S. Commerce Department building in Washington, D.C. The records administrator of the census suggests, in 1932, that the remaining files be extinguished. The Librarian of Congress agrees.

The paper trail, like the streets of the city, accumulates mystery.

Minnie's name is listed on Julius's death certificate. "Single, married, or divorced (write the word): Widower. If married, widowed, or divorced, husband of: Minnie Moskowitz."

On the fourth of June 1900, Nathan Weiss visits the rented house of Julius and Minnie Moskowitz at 324 Montrose Street, exactly five blocks from Julius's old peddler stand in the Washington Market. The house is across the street from a lumberyard. Weiss is a census enumerator. The Moskowitzes are the forty-first family Weiss has visited since June 2. The census taker notes that Julius arrives in the United States in 1888; this is one year before the confrontation at Love of Mercy synagogue. Minnie, or Minie, as Weiss records, arrives in the United States in 1890, a year after the religious Jews assault her husband on the holy day (negating the imagined scene of the night before, above). I should correct Minnie's persona: Here only a year, Julius, and look at all the trouble you're in!

Like Julius, she is born in 1864, in February. They marry at 17. By 1900 she has given birth eight times; five children survive: Janie (16), Dora (14), Mary (12), Harry (6), Raphael (4). Harry and Raphael are born in the United States. Harry must be conceived just after Julius's release from jail.

I mark this moment of the census, June 4, 1900. Eight people live in Minnie and Julius's house on Montrose Street, including a twenty-year-old boarder, Bertine Glasman, a shirt maker. The house is at once rundown and proud. It is about fifty years old already, I calculate, noting a row of buildings shown there in the 1862 atlas. The profile of that row matches the houses indicated in the 1895 atlas. The house probably does not have indoor plumbing. The rooms are small. The plaster is filthy, black in some places. Yet Minnie keeps it up. She doesn't work outside the house. Eleven people, members of the Melicson family from Russia and a boarder, also a shirt maker, live next door, to the east. The boarder's name is Rosie Goldberg. She is eighteen. She probably travels to and from work with Bertine Glasman, just two years older. At 326 Montrose, to the west, reside Daniel and Sarah O'Connel, born in Ireland, and their five children, age eight and under. O'Connel is a day laborer, frequently out of work.

All together, four people in the Moskowitz house bring in income. Janie is a cigar maker, Dora a dressmaker, and Mary goes to school. Julius lists his profession as "Watchman," the same profession held by Adolph Waechter at the time of his death in 1937. Julius lists zero as the number of months in the year he has been out of work.

1900 City Directory: Moskowitz Julius, inspector, h 324 Montrose.

"Inspector" is a more formal version of "watchman."

Minnie has no profession.

1900 U.S. Census:

	Can read.	Can write.	Can speak English.
Julius	yes	yes	yes
Minie [*sic*]	no	no	no

Julius is sent to County Prison in 1892 to learn a lesson: you can't shame others and get away with it, especially if you don't believe in God. Janie is eight, Dora is six, Mary is four. Three children don't survive to 1900. We might presume at least one of them dies while Julius is in jail, punishment enough. Minnie gives birth in January 1884, August 1885, and October 1887, and not again until August 1893. Not a living child again until August 1893. But this is a child of freedom.

With Julius in County Prison, Minnie receives aid from the Jewish anarchists—Pioneers of Freedom or Knights of Freedom or both—and, says Weinberg, four additional dollars a week from the Single Taxers (who believe in equal distribution of land value), "all together eight dollars, which is more than her husband ever earned working in a shop."

28

On August 6, I receive a letter from Armen Terzian, the developer of the apartment house, on crisp white stationery: "On successive days, I personally have attempted to contact you by phone, at both your office and mobile numbers, and by email . . ."

"Has anyone tried to call?" I ask Nadia in a hollow voice. I haven't stopped paying her and she hasn't stopped coming into work.

I read, "Please schedule a time to present your design for the project . . ."

"Have you spoken to anyone?"

"Failure to set up this meeting will . . ."

Nadia breaks the silence that now permeates our office. "I have told you about my uncle?"

"The one who went to jail? . . . You mentioned him. Why?"

"Why do I ask or why does he keep screwing up?"

"I'm not sure."

"Because he stopped living in reality."

"—"

"Why did we take this commission?"

"Because I said something that excited Terzian . . . Because two years ago I won an award . . ."

"My uncle has bankrupted my father."

"I convinced him he could make money and build something that matters."

"Not once, but twice. He is sick. I love him but he is sick."

"When you first walked in this office you said you wanted to build something that mattered, and I—"

"What does that letter say? Is it a threat? Have they paid you? Are they threatening to pull the contract? The one thing my uncle doesn't seem to ever learn is that there are consequences. It's as if he has no judgment. He was born without judgment, my father says. He was born without shame."

I crumple the letter. I toss it softly toward the trashcan.

"The building should look like it comes out of the ground, like it has grown like a tree," I say, absently. "Not like it is sitting on top of the ground or as if the ground is of merely one dimension."

29

KIDS AGAIN wake me up. They are playing baseball with a plastic bat and a foam ball. Who knows how many there are? I can hear only one; I can also hear the puff of the ball. His voice alone. He moves the other kids around the phantom field. At 417 S. 49th, in the neighborhood called Cedar Park, there is a tree outside our window, and others on the block. Eva and I share a twin-sized bed tucked into the wall, "among the cedar trees," we sometimes joke. The trees guard us, we decide, and protect us from evil forces. Outside noises don't penetrate the room though we keep the lone window open even in winter. Eva says she needs to feel the wind on her face to brush away the clutter in her head.

She needs to sleep with the window open to brush away the clutter that is me, sleeping right beside her. Lying in bed in the imaginary cedar forest, she says she loves me so much she can't think clearly.

When she returns to the house in early November 1990, she has cut her hair (in retrospect I align Eva with Julius's comrade Natasha Notkin). The short hair frames her cinnamon eyes; it naturally balances her strong hands and clear proportions. I say I am in favor. Uncluttered now, she doesn't answer.

In my copy of *Repetition*, I make some marks in blue and some in black. The blue ones, I surmise, I make in the days before Eva runs from my proposal; the black ones after. In pencil, I add new marks to page one hundred fifty-five, in the "Report by Constantin Constantius." "Everything has its time in youth, and what has had its time then has it again in later life." I underline this, and for added emphasis place two exclamation points in the margin.

Eva decides she will convert a storage closet connected to Reginald's bedroom into her own room. She approaches the project with a clear mission; by the end of the day, Saturday, November 3, 1990, Eva has given herself a place to sleep alone.

Outside my bedroom window, one of the boys has fallen. He is hurt. The singular voice of the lead boy, Devon, is silent. Now everything is silent. Light infatuates the room.

An hour and a half later, I rise out of the subway at Lombard-South.

Even despite Nadia's questions it hasn't occurred to me that I might be, according to bloodlines, related to Julius Moskowitz.

One day in 1932 this subway station opens. Julius, do you take a ride on the inaugural day? To get to the station would have required a streetcar ride of seven blocks and then a short walk, or perhaps a trip on a second streetcar. Perhaps you decide to join the throngs riding north to City Hall.

The staircase is a bridge between worlds. An Argentinian film portrays the life of a Buenos Aires subway custodian. He lives underground. He mops and cleans the station bathroom. The lamp flickers. The water pools, the grime collects as in a river delta. Mopping is Sisyphean, and yet the subway can't function without it. This subway station probably has a custodian, but I don't see anyone but the fare collector in the booth.

Water has pooled at the base of the stairs to the street. It hasn't rained. The sun is bright; it carves a yellow triangle on the wall.

Nadia, in a final act before going to Paris to see her father, has furnished me with documents. I carry a roll, in a rubber band, under my arm. The rest, neatly bound, are in my case. It is Saturday.

I imagine Julius walking from his house at 513 Carpenter Street, the address that's on his death certificate, to the subway station. He is sixty-eight years old. Minnie is Julius's wife, but she hasn't any interest in the new subway station. He walks alone. His knees are stiff. His mind is loose. He has lived here in Philadelphia for forty-four years. It doesn't matter to him why or why not. Moskowitz, the Internet tells me, is derived from Moshke, Moses, son of Moses. It hasn't anything to do with Moscow. It doesn't mean Muscovite. For forty-five of my own years, I have cultivated a misunderstanding. Eva, in 1990, calls me her Muscovy duck. Reginald and I talk incessantly of our Moscow, because if I am to return home, he is to come with me. The son of Moses crosses to Bainbridge Street, through a doorway into his past self, and hardly notices. A crowd has formed; he presses along, careful not to go too fast. Minnie has warned him about the danger of the crowd. The subway station is opening a generation behind schedule. The crowd accepts this with the pride of suffering. The joy is derisive.

I undo his walk from the subway station down South Street. At 6th I cross to Bainbridge. The workers have finished removing the Hebrew letters from the old synagogue. Cement smothers their ghosts.

The letters had lasted from 1905, more than a century. But is it dishonest to impugn the developer who is turning the synagogue into apartments for removing the letters? After all, the letters themselves are ghosts—of a people who have moved on. The congregation B'Nai Reuben, the first to construct a new synagogue building in the Jewish quarter, abandoned it in 1956, only fifty-two years after the founders laid the cornerstone. We might imagine a train of station wagons fleeing the city, starting in the mid-1950s and continuing for a quarter century, Jews banishing themselves to the suburbs.

Once you leave, how can you assume others will care to preserve your memory?

I am heading for the spot in the parking lot where Eva and I waited in the cold for Reginald to return with cash, where hours later he rapped on the window, a strange, attractive woman a foot or two behind. I check my watch. Walking from the subway toward the parking lot, I recite lines of passion and purity. I imagine what my father would do. With the sound of my footsteps on early fallen leaves, I speak, in my head, in clear, deliberate phrases, as if I am speaking to an idiot. Terzian corrects my tone. I allow it; I've been disrespectful. I tell him I am overcome with a desire to savor our meeting. I pay attention to his darting eyes, his hairy ears, the precise part of his hair. I unravel Nadia's carefully rendered plans on the hood of his Audi. I start with floor plans. I trace the arc of our thinking as if I am telling a story. I talk about the river, the city, the neighborhood, and the street. I talk about the actual ground. I stamp my foot for emphasis. I rub my hand over the cracked asphalt as if rubbing an infant's back. I ask if he has questions. Do you follow? He doesn't answer. I go on about cigar factories, synagogues, Irish cops, distilleries. I recall for him Weinberg's story about the cooperative shoe store on South Street, and later, the cooperative bakery, "the dream of a future society." I point to South Street. A building has values, it has memories, it has a voice. I will take a full half hour to lay this out, I tell myself. I imagine sweeping the pages of the plan as a great blue heron strokes its wings. Terzian's skin flakes. He scratches his knuckles.

On the spot where Eva says her head spins, across the double-wide chasm of Bainbridge, there is Julius, who believes neither in God nor in a state of future rewards and punishments, in mid-performance. I look out as if through a distant mirror. My hands—they are empty. There are no plans. I haven't even brought my leather case. But where is Terzian? I ask myself in a laconic voice. He won't dare stand me up.

30

ARMEN TERZIAN isn't here. I walk the inside of the parking lot as if tracing the lines of an asterisk, back and forth, center out, turn, walk away. Then the perimeter, along the uneven pavement, where I get my belt loop caught on a pin sticking out of a pole, the kind that once carried electrical current to the trolleys that made their turnaround a block away near our old bar, around the horse fountain with the engraving "drink gentle friend." The trolley hasn't run along Bainbridge in fifty years. Julius, are you there, just across the way through the oak and maple trees and the cheap aluminum fence? Your back is to me. Anyway, your attention is fixed on the words of Most; it must take all your concentration to ignore the shouts and tumbling hands . . .

They still haven't fixed the "park" that replaces the Washington Market. "A line of sad little trees." "Am I to meet Terzian?" I type into a text to send to Nadia, then delete. I begin again, so as to sound steadier: "The Terzian meeting is supposed to be now?" I recognize this sounds nearly as confused. My thumb stumbles across the keyboard. Delete. Delete. Delete.

"Nadia is in Paris," I say aloud, to no one. Sweat drips off my body to the pavement.

I'll build whatever you wish, I say to Terzian. My voice has a troubling, hollow, sycophantic tone. You read me aloud what you want and I'll draw it, like a town scribe. I'll draw it exactly to your specifications.

No, no. What I want to say is that a great building might acknowledge the layers of people who have been here before, take into account their lives and their imprint on the street just as it relents to the touch of the people who inhabit today. It's an absurd thought, really, if you think about matters from a practical perspective, but anarchists aren't practical thinkers. After all, you can't recreate the past. To do so is lazy. To do so is an affront to the profession of architecture. It's almost sinful. Terzian removes a handkerchief from his pocket and blows his nose. I take it as a gesture of empathy. His father won't condone our meeting. Imagine coming all this way into the city to meet an architect in the baking sun, on broken asphalt, with dust and exhaust in the air. He won't condone it, but he doesn't have to know, even if nothing comes of it and Armen has to hire one of the hacks who already work for his father. The old man doesn't have to know. I glance at Armen's rumpled face, old before his time. I brush a speck of dust from his shoulder.

"Is he coming," I manage to text to Nadia. Can she receive texts in Europe? What time is it in Paris? I can't possibly do the math. I hit send. Then I sense air and only air, as if sending the text has opened a door to an infinite horizon. Even Julius disappears.

Even a gesture can be misinterpreted and misunderstood. I don't know how Nadia will ever forgive me.

31

A YOUNG MAN ANSWERS when I dial the number on the For Sale sign. How many bedrooms, I want to know. And bathrooms? Has the kitchen been updated? The young man asks if I am looking to invest in property or if I am searching for a house for myself. I really don't know, I say. The idea that a building can respond to people, living or dead—it's not the right time to explain. My lack of answer confuses him, but he quickly overcomes his hesitation. After all, he really doesn't care. We arrange a time for a walk-through.

In my walks from the Baltimore Avenue trolley, I assign labels to the houses and apartment buildings as I pass, all of them built between 1880 and 1910. This one is "courageous"; that one is "burly"; the one across the street has "quiet strength." Our house, I decide, is a shy beauty; the name alone invites a memory of Eva, with her short hair and her blue backpack, sitting at the bakery table and writing in her notebook intently. The young man tries to lead me from room to room. The theme of his sales pitch is potential; that's why he wants to know my intentions. If I say I wish to live here with my wife and children (should they exist), he will point up all the advantages for an ideal domestic life; if I say I want to rent it to a group or divide it up into small apartments, he will pull out plans, already drawn up, that show how it can be done.

The young man keeps getting bunched up behind me as I stop in odd places. I stand in the first-floor hallway; the hair on the top of my head, the reach of my eyes, the position of my ears, all this gathers information past, repeating back onto the present. Eventually the young man retreats to the front living room; he sits below the English windows, for the built-in seat is still there. Who lives here now? Graduate students, I surmise, from China or Taiwan probably. The kitchen smells of rice vinegar. But no one is home.

Whatever on the surface has changed—drywall over plaster, cheap gray carpet in places over hardwood that I once painted in a weekend frenzy, a newborn closet, a green countertop—drains immediately from vision. I stop in the doorway of my room and I wonder, if she were there too, would Eva stop, would Eva help me contemplate the scene? I recognize now how thoroughly I've erased her all these years, like letters chiseled off a building. This is the first I conceive of her as a mature adult, a free element in the world. What kind of life does she have? Is she married? Is work in the law fulfilling? For a moment or two, I indulge myself by thinking that with a close inspection of the woodwork and the windowsills, by sliding the window open and closed, by looking under the tapestry (that appears, by the design of it, to carry religious meaning that I cannot understand) covering the ornate mahogany closet, I will discover the lost source of my shame, the truth of our lost love.

A voice stirs me from the dream, Harris's voice signifying that dinner is ready. It's the young man. He wants to know if I have any questions.

Upstairs, I duck into Reginald's room—his lair—inside the front eave. I trip on the futon. Here is the doorway to Eva's room. But where? Like a lizard, I paw the wall and then creep around to the other side. I can't approach it. I gaze back at the stairs and follow the line through Reginald's room to her door; back out, I try again. I measure the space, stair landing to the back wall of the house and then forward to the back wall of his room. This is the storage closet she turns into a bedroom, but the space, demarcated in space, as any room is, by its structure, is gone. Whoever has erased it is playing a trick.

32

REGINALD WILL COME with me to River Road, to my childhood home, to have Christmas 1990 with my father. Larry cooks for the three days and we eat for eight or nine hours. Does Reginald bring the clove cigarettes for old times? Clove cigarettes go along with the Christmas ham. I climb the stairs to the third-floor landing—I want to see if he is ready to go. Eva blocks my way. She isn't aggressive; her hands and eyes carry a pitying air. I wish her a relaxing break. This is the most I've said to her in a month. "You think this is about you," she says. "And so you wonder what you're supposed to do, you beg me to tell you what to do."

"Not really—"

"This doesn't have anything to do with you."

33

THINGS HAPPEN in place. Does the place remember?

I have to remind it of what it doesn't remember. I have to borrow memories.

Moskowitz leaves Moyamensing Prison before Christmas of 1892. Less than a year later, on November 19, H. H. Holmes is brought in on suspicion of insurance fraud and possibly murder. The arraignment is covered in the *New York Times*. Holmes doesn't mind his stay in Moyamensing. The writer Erik Larson, in *The Devil in the White City*, says that Holmes's cell is the prison's standard: nine by fourteen feet, whitewashed walls, high corner window with bars. There is a single electric lamp, "extinguished at nine o'clock each night."

Moyamensing is known for "extreme cleanliness, with floors and walls of dazzling white." I find this description of the prison in *Philadelphia Politics from the Bottom Up*, a biography of the ward boss William McMullen, the Irish king of Bainbridge Street, by Harry Silcox. In the years before Moskowitz arrived in the neighborhood, McMullen, an alderman, was a Moyamensing Prison inspector, sent in to make sure the prisoners were treated according to the rules, posted on the wall:

Keep your cells as clean as possible.
Make no unnecessary noise whatever.
Do not talk to anyone except keeper or inspector.
Do not write or make marks upon walls or floor.
Throw nothing down the pipe or out the ventilator.
Keep your bunk up during the day.
Do not smoke in your cell, or spit out the window.
Any infraction of the above will be punished by depriving
  you of your food or confining you to the dark cell.

In 1900, seven years after he leaves Moyamensing Prison, Moskowitz lists his profession in the city directory as "inspector." I begin to feel it's possible that the formerly imprisoned radical turned religious man could become a prison inspector. Later he may even be a prison guard. In 1916 he puts himself in the city directory as "deputy sheriff." Is this how the anarchist repudiates his beliefs, makes up for his shame, by turning opposite? Julius, do you favor protecting the prisoners or upholding the rule of law or the political machine?

Holmes charms the prison guards. He dresses in street clothes. He wears a watch. He sends out for food and newspapers.

Frank Geyer is the detective on Holmes's case. Geyer wears a "walrus mustache." In 1896, the year Holmes is executed by hanging, Geyer publishes a book on the investigation and the trial, *The Holmes-Pitezel Case: A History of the Greatest Crime of the Century*. Holmes, observes Geyer, "is greatly given to lying with a sort of florid ornamentation, and all of his stories are decorated with flamboyant draperies, intended by him to strengthen the plausibility of his statements. In talking, he has the appearance of candor, becomes pathetic at times when pathos will serve him best, uttering his words with a quaver in his voice, often accompanied by a moistened eye, then turning quickly with a determined and forceful method of speech, as if indignation or resolution had sprung out of tender memories that had touched his heart."

Julius isn't Holmes; he could not be so disingenuous.

34

MOSKOWITZ WEARS his prison suit. It is spotless. He sits in the lamplight. He crouches in the corner, low to the ground, listening to the hum.

What are the daily degradations? Can't speak. Can't move. Can't see Minnie or Dora or Janie or Mary. Prenner is there and Gillis and Jacobs. These are your comrades. In prison on bogus charges, your anger moors. Moskowitz observes Prenner striving. He meets with strangers who visit, who hand him books. Does Prenner repudiate the movement or the movement him? Moskowitz blames the movement, for it's the movement that has made Prenner a climber; it has given him power.

Moskowitz, who doesn't believe in God, sits in the corner of his cell and thinks. The government inspector enters your village. He spends days fabricating a report. The Jews, he says, speaking in his own head to the Czar himself, are saying outlandish things. The Jews won't follow orders—the clear rules you set out, dear ruler, to protect the Russian people. Even the Russian people here in Romania, my Czar, one day they will be Russian. Romania, indeed, is where Mosko-

151

witz is from. On every government form after the 1910 census, including his own death certificate, he indicates:

Place of Birth: Romania

The walls are thick, Erik Larson, born in Brooklyn, says of Moyamensing Prison, in *The Devil in the White City*. The thick walls insulate against the summer heat but not the humidity, which clings "like a cloak of moist wool." Through the thick walls Moskowitz can barely make out the Hebrew chant of another prisoner. He hears it not with his ears but with his guts.

Inside his cell, Holmes complains that "The great humiliation of feeling that I am a prisoner is killing me far more than any other discomforts I have to endure." *The great humiliation of feeling that I am a prisoner*: this is the humiliation of the vanquished, a savage tied to a tree.

The Hebrew that Moskowitz hears with his gut deepens the humiliation, but it also beckons like freedom.

Holmes is a wildcard of a man, amoral. He eats away at the world according to hunger alone.

Once a day, in the morning, a clergyman comes to deliver a sermon. He stands in the cellblock and raises his voice so that each prisoner in his cell, behind the iron door, on his iron cot, can hear. The clergyman says: You are imprisoned by your own bad thoughts, your own savage instincts. The free man, the Christian man, restrains himself. He offers a book of scripture to anyone who can read. Julius, will you take one?

Humiliation, to be brought low, like talking to an imaginary man.

Prison humiliates the free man by denying his soul. It denies his religion.

We imagine Julius Moskowitz outside his stall in the Washington Market, October 1889. He is reciting Most's "Anarchist Communism," translated into Yiddish. It has just appeared in print. Moskowitz keeps it in his pocket. Moskowitz crumples it in his hand, softly, as one caresses the ear of a dog. "Is anarchism desirable? Well, who does not seek freedom? What man, unless willing to declare himself in bondage, would care to call any control agreeable? Think about it!" Moskowitz, too, is a savage chained to a tree. In his cell, separated from Most, a Hebrew chant slides in.

Prenner, Gillis, Jacobs, and Moskowitz: they inhabit the same cellblock, the cellblock for nonviolent criminals. Prenner, the organizer, the strategist, receives missives from the capitalists who had him locked up. A smart guy like you is wasting his time with these radical ideas. You can be a great leader of the community. You don't need to suffer. We'll pay for your college courses if you come to our side.

Who will call on you, Julius?

You can't humiliate a man for his beliefs, you can't make fun, says Judge Arnold. This is Moskowitz's crime: humiliation. On the day of Yom Kippur, 1889, he brings the religious men so low they abandon themselves. They lose their self-restraint. They behave like wild children. Then they take revenge. Humiliation is a danger.

This is Moskowitz's punishment: humiliation.

Less than human, you anarchist.

Moskowitz sits in the corner of his cell, the bull waiting, imagining mercy.

35

It's been an hour since I filled out the request form at the City Archive. The air conditioning washes over my feet. I look over at the attendant. She is on the phone. The archivist wheels in books for other researchers. Am I invisible? Have I done something wrong? Am I allowed to speak? Can I walk around?

Silent, I strain my neck to see if someone is coming. I turn the other way to see the clock. The air conditioning tastes sour. The sun outside is like a glowing fuse. Another fifteen minutes pass. I don't dare move. Downstairs, the subway rumbles like a tired beast.

In my frustration, I decide to text Cecil. Maybe now it's time to take a break, swim in the ocean. It's impossible to get anything done in August. I text: "I'm ready to go. Any day."

As before, he texts back immediately, as if not a single second has passed. "Moscowitz! You've come to your senses. But guess what! So have I."

"What?"

"I'm leaving for Kathmandu."

"When?"

154

"2 days."

"Comin back?"

"No return ticket."

"Congratulations."

"You want my mother's #? She'll cook for you. Plenty of room in the house."

"Oh thanks. No, no. Kathmandu, you weren't kidding."

"I'll let you know how it goes."

The attendant gets off the phone. About my request . . . She is polite but guarded. She promises to check with the archivist. She lifts the phone receiver as if to dial and then she sets it down. "As soon as she's back from lunch," she says. She's wearing a wool sweater to protect against the excess cold.

"I guess I don't understand how things work here," I say.

A while later the archivist appears. I ask about the materials. She stares off at the window. "Your materials are right here," she says in a detached tone. She puts her hand on a file cart behind me. I've been imprisoned by my own confusion. She takes each mud-red leather-bound book and drops it on my table. Dust jets into my tongue and teeth. She keeps her gaze fixed on the window. Make no claim on me.

I approach the books as if they guard a secret. I clear my throat, begin my search of prison reports: reports of incidents, reports of illness and death, reports on sanitation and food. Everything is scrupulously documented. This is the secret of good government. Even a prison must operate for the good of all. But nothing I seek is here. These reports are from the 1830s. I feel like a child who has accidentally sat on the lap of the wrong mother. I close the books with a thud. Dust sprays, leather chips like broken snow-packed leaves under booted foot. I try to rake the detritus into a pile. My cheeks must be smeared red. I keep rubbing my face and hands, kicking bent leg and rocking like a holy fool.

"Annual report inspectors county prison Philadelphia moyamensing," entered as a Google Books search, returns "Second Annual Message of John Weaver, Mayor of the City of Philadelphia, with the Annual Reports of David J. Smyth, Director of the Department of Public Safety, and of the Chiefs of Bureaus Constituting Said Department, for the Year Ending December 31, 1904." The digitized book comes from the University of Chicago Library, Class 352.074, Book P53, Compliments of John Weaver, Mayor. The Bureau of Boiler Inspection charges County Prison, Moyamensing, $48.10 for, presumably, boiler inspection. There are similar books online for 1903 and 1937. The "First Annual Report of the Philadelphia County Prison, 1848," the property of Harvard College Library, notes, in its introduction on the mandate of the inspector, that the aim of imprisonment is reform of the criminal. "Thus it is that humanity, as well as the law, is alike interested in the welfare of the convict."

"There is at present quite a number of excellent books, forming indeed a tolerable library, at the prison, furnished by the Prison Discipline Society, and other humane persons."

1861: "No case of insanity has occurred during the year, although the intellectuality of a large portion of the prisoners received, was of an unusually low grade."

1910: "There was an absence of that prison odor usually found in corridors and hallways of institutions, and the inmates have no cause for complaint."

The years of digitized reports skip around at random. 1880. 1932. 1837.

The Internet is like the city itself: half erased. Or rather, perhaps, half preserved.

The Prison Discipline Society, of Boston, Massachusetts, lists causes of mental illness among black prisoners. The leading cause is masturbation. This is 1844. "It does not appear that shutting men up in solitary cells and leaving them without much instruction, leads to reformation."

There is no inspection report online for 1891 or 1892 or 1893.

In 1894 Julius lives at 517 Carpenter Street, rear. His occupation, listed in the city directory: tailor. It isn't clear from the record that Julius has been a tailor before. We may be safe to surmise that Minnie is the tailor. While Julius is in prison, she receives eight dollars each week from his comrades. But she must take in work to feed her children. In 1894 Julius is out of jail, but he may also be out of work. "Tailor" protects Julius's standing.

In 1892, while Julius inhabits a cell in Moyamensing Prison, Minnie and her three daughters, Janie, Dora, and Mary, live at 429 Carpenter, on a tiny alley, "Young's Court," next to a coffee roaster. Their house is a ten-minute walk from the prison.

Does she walk, in a single straight line, down Passyunk Avenue for a chance to visit her husband? Illiterate and unable to speak English? We can't be sure. In the literature on the prison, there is no mention of visiting day.

The city accumulates its loss. Even as places are erased, the city remembers. The city will tell, as if whispering a secret. The fields and cemeteries that once surround the prison—or rather, the landscape the prison imposes itself on as soon as the immigrant workers haul the stone to the site, on the edge of the metropolis—is muzzled in the 1860s. Development comes. First small workshops and row houses replace the parade grounds and farms. Then iron foundries, paper factories, smokestacks. Then more row houses, the largest on the main numbered streets, the tiniest on alleys cut between them, replace the jumble. My perception from walking these streets is of a cityscape in constant tension, like a jigsaw puzzle a child has put together wrong, but in the 1890s all but the prison is new, even, and rigid. A mural nearby records the scene at this time, singular figures of immigrants occupying discrete space along the sidewalk, like actors on a stage. Nostalgia is powerful. It dyes the visual frame and demands we acquiesce. Calabrian and Sicilian immigrants assume the rigid landscape around the prison. They attack it with their culture as the landscape gives way.

Moskowitz is in his 1830s cell as this is happening. The walls are thick. It's distorting to be stuck inside another time. Julius, whom do you think about? Janie, Dora, and Mary? Do you arrange them neatly in your mind? Do you dream of a son?

A stone wall encloses the prison block. Lads play in its shadow in the ancient lithograph. They make up stories about the people inside. The wall is visible in the street atlas, double stutter lines to indicate the thickness. The prison is like a powerful repelling magnetic force that pushes Reed Street into an upside down V. The main part of the prison wall is white marble. White is light. White is hope. Walter, the architect, wants his fortress to foam like a cloud. The northern end is for debtors at first and then, later, women. It is brownstone, cut, like the white stone, into long rectangular blocks. The brownstones remain, three rectangles tall, forming the base of chain-link fence at the northwest corner of the prison site. Interior layers of stone follow Reed Street along the upside down V, on either side of the brownstone section. This dwarf wall is the only physical remnant of Moyamensing Prison.

I flood the present-day street map across the 1895 atlas. The ghost form of the white prison holds its ground.

Moskowitz leaves the courthouse at 6th and Chestnut, beneath the tower of Independence Hall, in a horse-drawn police carriage. The prisoners are all together. They do not speak. The others look to Prenner. He looks away. Moskowitz is still. His eyes are blue. He is afraid to move. From inside the police carriage he can't see the frothy fortress. He's never seen it from the outside. Though sturdy, he casts a small figure. Even in his tiny cell, Moskowitz is nothing. He feels himself a rat.

He has no plans for his time in prison, no sense of mission. Will he work making shoes? It might alleviate the boredom. Moskowitz has never really liked to work. Time will make its own way, he thinks. Time is effortless. It's us, with our kinetic consciousness, that bog it down. History is like a mirror. It allows us to reflect on ourselves. Before the mirror—before the discovery of a still pond or puddle—you can't reflect. You can only grub forward. Before history there is only today and tomorrow. Tomorrow presses on today. It's the reason for today. History, once it's discovered, presses back. It demands something of today—either forget it or duplicate it. All along I've had the feeling that Moskowitz isn't the type to get bogged down with anything. That's the irony. Without meaning to he's created a mess for himself. Circumstances, the past piling up on the present, have him trapped in a nine by fourteen cell. But why should I imagine Julius as passive? Is it because I feel this way about myself?

I must have it wrong. He doesn't like to work, but he feels passionately. He acts without reflection, as if on fire. Circumstances will propel such a man. Circumstances will get such a man into trouble. Open, searching, supple, this is Moskowitz. His nose has been broken. His English is blunt. His Romanian Yiddish rises and falls like the music of Verdi. In prison he grows resentful of Prenner. Gillis disgusts him—he hasn't earned his imprisonment. Only Jacobs, the cigar maker, offers comfort, but Jacobs is morally weak. He has no backbone. While pamphleting it is Jacobs who strikes the Jew with his *tefillin*, but he hasn't ever admitted it. Moskowitz plays that event in his mind. When he does so, sitting in his cell, he sees Jacobs's rabid face—a face of cruelty.

Cruelty, he thinks, is dishonesty.

He thinks of his Yom Kippur prayer, 1889. He wonders if he has been cruel. He tries to recall the faces of the religious men. Are they the cruel ones? When they attacked him he went blind. Now, in the prison cell, he feels their shaking fingers claw at his coat, but he cannot see their faces.

Hours go by. Days. Once, he tells the guard he wants to

work. Where do I go? The next morning the guard escorts him to the shoemaking shop. The foreman will tell you what to do. The three others are there. None of them speak to him. They won't look at him. It's as if Moskowitz is invisible.

36

THE DOOR BETWEEN my private office and the studio is open.
And I turn in my chair and look at the old bakery table. I have
a sense of where it might go.

I dial Terzian's office, put the phone to my ear, and wait
for his secretary to answer. I identify myself and ask to speak
to Terzian.

Her voice is blank at first, as if she's never heard of me.
"Moscowitz, the architect."

"Who?"

Am I mumbling or dreaming?

"The architect. Bainbridge Street." Soon I recognize she's
acting out her own frustration. How unprofessional, I think
at first, and then I smile. I even laugh into the phone. "OK,
maybe I should try his cell phone?"

"Try it," she says. I detect a slight laugh, with or at me I'm
not sure.

He picks up immediately. Terzian isn't interested in games.
This is the first thing he says.

"No games," I promise.

"OK, and the plans?" His voice is clipped. He isn't calm.

"The plans."

"I want to go over them with you before the community meeting."

"I have a vision for the site," I say.

"That's why I hired you."

"But I'm afraid it can't be brought to life. This is why I called." I pause, thinking of Eva and me in the car in the frigid darkness . . . of Popkin staring at the lot, dreaming . . . "It might be better, for now, at least, if it were to remain a parking lot."

Has he hung up? Yes, the line is dead. But when had he stopped listening?

37

Nadia accompanies me to a second showing of 417 S. 49th Street. On the trolley she tells me about her trip to Paris. Her father is considering moving back to Beirut, she says. He's had enough of French cruelty. "This kind of thing never used to bother him," she says. He feels invisible. "When you get old you just want to be who you are."

"I don't know what I'm going to do," I say to myself. I'll pay her as long as I can. There is enough in the account. When I sell my house . . .

"I think he's making a mistake. You don't ever go back," she says.

"Who?" I try to recall whom she means.

"My father!"

"Reasons aren't always clear." I manage a smile. The trolley shakes through an underground zigzag to reach 36th and Sansom. Often I trace the tunnel lines in my head.

"Why are we going to see this house?" she asks. Her voice is direct.

"A client has asked me to assess it."

"For a restoration? We don't do much restoration work."
The use of "we" comforts me.

"Maybe it's a resurrection instead. Things have to be torn down before they can be rebuilt."

"Grandma Malakeh again."

"What?"

"You're a mystic."

Should I tell her everything, about the state of my mind, about my obsessive chase of Moskowitz, about my search for my own lost truth? At Baltimore Avenue the trolley comes up from the tunnel; the sun casts a harsh glare on Nadia's face. "If a house has a soul already, even a dark one, how does an architect respond? Gutting it? No, that's not the answer," I say. A man in the seat in front of us goes back and forth between two phones he's fidgeting with. In between them he sits outstretched like a live wire. I'm afraid he's going to kill us.

When I ask Nadia, in order to distract myself, if she dreams of living in Paris, she says that would mean choosing: Lebanese or French. "Here I'm allowed to be double, so it doesn't matter. I'm just another American."

At 49th Street we get cardamom ice cream at Little Baby's. Naturally we submit to opposing views of gentrification. She sees nothing wrong with the neighborhood becoming "nicer." I ask, "But what has been lost?"

At my request, inside 417 S. 49th Street, Nadia makes rough sketches of the house. I sit on a white plastic chair. I've read somewhere that this is the most reproduced furniture item in the world. In this room, at the bakery table, I scribble "Eternal resurrection" in blue ink below a star on a page of *Repetition* that I fold down—page one hundred forty-nine. "Eternal resurrection," Eva says, her voice in memory softer, perhaps, sometime before October 11, 1990. The star sits on top of a stick, like a magic wand. Sitting here with her head resting on her fist, Eva is yet again teaching me Kierkegaard's meaning of repetition. Now I think I've got it. With my pencil I underline (and recite the words to myself in a sing-song voice, words we once said to each other about sex, which we pursue with repeated hunger, never sated): "The dialectic of repetition is easy, for that which is repeated has been—otherwise it could not be repeated—but the very fact that it has been makes the repetition into something new."

38

A YEAR AFTER my encounter with Genevieve and the anarchists of Baltimore Avenue, I bring someone new into the house. I do this because:

> Nicole is lively and rich.
> She chain-smokes and plays poker and I find this infatuating.
> I discover a taste for bourbon.
> I feel I no longer need to sleep.
> I want to provoke Eva.

To bring Nicole into the house, to sleep with her, to play music, to sit on the lawn and get high is to assert an unimaginable cruelty. Reginald tells me so. "You have no right . . ." Abigail and Harris turn me invisible.

I am blind to good sense and humiliation.

Nadia comes down the stairs followed by the young man. I close my eyes as if listening for a distant echo.

Nadia says she's sketched all three floors but she can't figure out a section of the third floor. "It's as if it's there and it's not there," she says. "We'd have to break the wall."

The young man, trying to be accommodating in the hope of a sale, says he will see what he can do. "The house is ideally situated . . ."

The young man's insistent angling disguised as idle chatter induces me to close my eyes again and wait until Nadia interrupts. I want to hear her voice take form in the volume of this room. Then she remembers to ask to see the basement. I recall the same acquisitive tone, a tone in the perfect middle range, self-inventing but hardly dreamy; I try to possess that voice on the night of October 11, 1990, but it gets away from me.

39

NADIA'S SKETCH of the third floor shows where Eva's room is but isn't. She uses dotted lines to extend the space from Reginald's room. One day, in early May 1991, Eva invites me in. The books and notebooks are stacked, the clothes are folded in a pile (she has no dresser). I regret she's had to sleep in this airless place; there is no window. "We leave the door open," she says, "Reg shares his air."

We fumble in the pleasantry.

She asks about Nicole. What music does she like, what books, what's her major? When I answer—Springsteen, Cheever, Chemistry—she lights a cigarette. I've never seen her smoke before.

"It's serious?"

I shrug. My eyes pick up things. Underwear, a key ring, the dress I'd given her on her twentieth birthday. *Architecture of Rome.*

"I got that for you," I say, "since we planned to go."

"I can't go, obviously, I have no money. Got to save it for law school, anyway."

"Law school."

"Are you going to go anyway?" she asks urgently. "Maybe with Nicole?"

I've made her needy. She's been like this for a while, unlike herself, someone else. I have no plans, I tell her.

She comes closer.

I guard my repulsion. I used to say, "I can never live without you." But she's exhausted the love, dried it out trying to unclutter her head or heart. She's entitled, I would tell myself. But she stayed shut away in her room and I have shut her out.

Nicholas, can you understand what it feels like to be shut out? Locks changed? It's humiliating. We live in the same house, inside the same walls. We walk the same stairs.

It's cruel.

Now it's over. Don't make her try to pick the lock, crawl back inside, I tell myself. Don't double-humiliate her. You wouldn't do that, would you?

And you, Eva, why are you willing to betray yourself now, lose your control? Have I provoked you? The night you ran from me down the alley next to our bar, did you lose control, did something unfurl? But weren't you also asserting control? "Taking back my life," you said, in a meditative voice, when finally we talked about it.

And what am I doing playing along, rubbing your shoulders, smelling your hair? Have I come into your room intentionally to seduce you? Am I so cruel? Or is your reaction, or mine, to our bodies in such close proximity inadvertent, as if it can't be helped?

I stand up to leave. No, really, I have to go.

Her cinnamon eyes have darkened, black bags, heavy eyelids. Have there been tears? She reaches up, with a pathetic look, to offer me a drag of her cigarette, as if there's nothing left but despair. "I've been rereading Kierkegaard. You know I was the one who was supposed to find someone else, I think his name is 'Johan.'"

"There is time," I think to say, and tell myself to open the door, and don't. Reject the cigarette. Instead: "It's much quieter up here than downstairs."

"You turned it on me. You really did. Of course the poet is a deceiver."

"I'm no poet," I smile. "Anyway, he's deceiving in order to protect—I think you explained that to me. Wily Søren."

She goes to close the door, cigarette in mouth. Whatever she does, she learns to do it with an intensity of feeling and a capacity for adaptation. A feeling of fresh love and tenderness stirs inside me, like a tiny bug I feel crawling around inside my shirt but can't find. I push myself toward her.

I've never known anyone as nakedly as Eva. She stands in front of the shut door and takes off her shirt.

Stop, Nicholas! No, but I don't stop. I push forward and she becomes passive, almost limp. She's letting this happen to her, and no mention of birth control, no concern about consequences of any kind. Am I going to tear out her heart? Can I be held responsible? Maybe I'm going to fuck her out of pity and self-hate, out of cruelty, or nostalgia, the memory of tenderness. I've done this to her, made her seduce me, made her betray herself.

Maybe I'm going to shame us both. While doing so, I'm going to take our love—love still breathing, perhaps—suffocate it and then erase it.

40

Moskowitz spends a few weeks in the prison shoemaking shop. He doesn't mind it, aside from the spring heat. He pounds heels. For a while, he doesn't look out the window into the courtyard. Why taste the air? But he can't help it, and once, on the way into the shop, he steals a glimpse at the sky.

He stops going to work. He pores over cruelty. This is the word in Yiddish, with Hebrew characters: אַכזאָריעס. *Akhzoryes*, cruelty, is a wall thicker than stone. It has nothing to do with belief.

Moskowitz tests himself again. On the morning of Yom Kippur, 1889, is he demonstrating cruelty? He is reading, standing and reading. It is a mockery, isn't it? And mockery is a kind of cruelty. He wishes he had the Most with him in prison. The German advocates violence, but violence isn't cruelty. Everyone should be free to follow his conscience. But he can't recall the words exactly. He wants to reread. He wants to assure himself. He looks around. The guard paces the cellblock. The guard isn't cruel. The guard's eyes flicker empathy and sadness. The guard thinks the prisoner always hurts himself, he can't help it. He undermines his own cause. The guard feels pity. He tries to help, but a man must help himself, take responsibility. Only the man himself can make the change. He is a firm believer in this philosophy. Moskowitz looks at the bars and the walls. He looks at the floor. He looks at his own thick, short fingers, the nails gray and puckered. Eight months in jail is nothing. But punishment isn't healing. Punishment isn't teaching.

Punishment may be stealing. Moskowitz concentrates on this for a while. The state stealing from the people, taking away their time. He wants to sleep, but the guard won't let him sleep. Punishment is just a guess. It is always arbitrary. It isn't sad and it isn't cruel.

41

WHY WON'T I let Nadia go? To keep her, perhaps that is cruel. What am I doing with her inside the house at 417 S. 49th Street? Do I seek an arbitrary pleasure, or a way to punish myself for the pain I caused Eva so long ago? But Nadia isn't Eva—she might be surprised to even know of Eva and the true reason I am having her trace the dimensions of the rooms and of the walls. Now, like Kierkegaard's poet, I have become a double deceiver.

And what am I doing blowing the Terzian commission, spending all my time on a double trail, it occurs to me again, of Moscowitz and Moskowitz? If I am making a turn in my life, repudiating all that I once believed so firmly that I must do, as if preordained, where will I go? Nothing feels tangible. I think of what I was asked to recite on my bar mitzvah, "the sum of the things for the tabernacle": a tangible world suffused with the presence of God. Yet it's me, inside 417 S. 49th Street, imposing meaning on mute and tangible things.

Architecture is tasteless to me now, probably because I have tried so hard to make it taste real, and all that must be authentic requires, perhaps counter-intuitively, precision of thought and execution. Precision comes from relentless pounding, probably over generations and centuries, and not from perfect conception or an individual's vision. Perhaps this is the basis of Nadia's point about the search for an answer. Tenacity comes from the outside, not from within. The pounding has exhausted me, no less because I can no longer be sure I am hitting the mark. I sit, in the white plastic chair of endless reproduction, in the room where I most love and admire Eva, and I close my eyes and I dream of escape. My mother, Hilda, dreams of that escape as my father pursues perfection in his kitchen. And then she runs.

I dream of footsteps over the bridge and across the Schuylkill River, the footsteps that take me out of Eva's room that day in early May 1991, from the lost space of my humiliation. I dream of the source of my present misery. Along the riverbank I discover a poet and an artist below the sculpture of the angels. The poet is Stephen Berg. He wears a hat. The artist is Thomas Chimes. He smiles gladly. I ask them what they're doing and they explain they're stenciling words onto the top of the concrete retaining wall along the river. I want to touch their shoulders. I want to absorb their presence, deep in meditative silence, into me.

"It's a profane prayer. Careful if you read it," says the poet, Berg, and I shyly listen. Words spread north and south, lingering with the river, and yet above it, as Chimes colors them in:

> help the mystery speak like a letter to an intimate friend
> and not hinder the sacred troubled beauty love is was will
> be love has shaken me like wind rushing down

Berg is a poet of poets. Egoless. He casts a net into their welkin of words. Theirs are his. His words are his and theirs, borrowed, shared. His poems are sediment. They form layers.

I am afraid to hover and watch the men work. I don't want to disturb or impose. Writing to the city—they are writing to the city, I discover, as a building might, as a building could. Yet in my shame I turn away, afraid of being overpowered. I realize then, for the humiliation of Eva, I will punish myself through isolation.

Leaving the poet and the artist, I go up from the river saturated in unease. Yet I am free, as free in this moment as I will be ever again. I can sense the freedom from here, from afar. Inside it, I can only guess. My feet quicken along the gravel path. The earth is supple in spring. It gives. The goose shit is green and black. The cherry blossoms, half darkened, hesitate. The angels hover. If I point to two moments of genuine inspiration toward architecture, I recall the view from the second-floor loft of the textile mill in Kensington, with Genevieve pilfering sweaters, and this one, observing two men listening to the city and recording their reaction, listening and giving, in repetition, listening and transforming what they hear into something new.

This original urge to architecture, born of shame: as Julius turned from prison to build his holy society.

Now, with the real estate agent hovering nearby, I sit in the dining room of the old house and recall myself leaving here for a new apartment, a tiny studio in another outlying district, Fairmount, the same part of the city where I live now. The studio apartment is freshly painted bright white. The smell of the fresh paint and the lacquer on the floor intoxicates. Sitting on the floor without any furniture, I page through the newspaper. The window behind me is open and I can hear the birds rattling around the brick patio below. I come across a headline, "Poem On Schuylkill Wall Has Gotten Even Deeper." Beyond the poem's first words, "How can you know what it means to be here," two hundred feet of it had fallen into the river. The retaining wall had given way.

Neither the poet Berg nor the artist Chimes seemed disturbed. Berg told the newspaper's reporter that the collapse "extends the meaning of the line." The poem is about higher power, letting go of will. With these words, in 1991, one hundred years after Julius is arrested for attempting to tear down the state and all authority, I set out, earnestly, idealistically, to build things up.

42

How can it be that there is a film called *Minnie and Moskowitz*? Cassavetes makes the movie in 1971, a few years before playing Nicky in Elaine May's *Mikey and Nicky*, shot on the desolate streets of the Jewish quarter. *Minnie and Moskowitz* and *Mikey and Nicky* share a volatile intensity. In *Minnie and Moskowitz*, Cassavetes plays the abusive married lover of Gena Rowlands (his real-life wife). But the film doesn't center on him. Rather, it's about the explosive relationship between Rowlands, as Minnie, whose apartment is filled with books and who works at the Los Angeles County Museum, and the gummed-up Moskowitz, who wears a walrus mustache, long hair in a pony tail, and parks cars for a living. Seymour Cassel plays Moskowitz. Minnie is mercurial. Her given name is Minerva. She doesn't know why she should stoop to Moskowitz's level. Moskowitz punches the wall when he is overwhelmed by feeling. "I know why I like you," she says. They are sitting at a hot dog stand on South Broadway in Downtown L.A. "You talk about practical things . . . you talk about getting fed . . . spending money."

"A lifetime of frustrated energy into a single deadly night." That is how the film critic Richard Brody describes *Mikey and*

Nicky. It is a summer night. Cassavetes and Peter Falk, playing Mikey, glisten with sweat. Erik Larson, in his book on H. H. Holmes, calls Philadelphia's summer humidity "notorious." The poet Berg says that when the air is "thick greasy," "every little thing feels difficult."

Every little thing . . . I begin to think every little thing must matter.

In 1998 Berg publishes *Shaving,* a book of prose poems. I find it at Robin's Bookstore. 1998 is the year I read Buzz Bissinger's new book *A Prayer for the City.* Everyone reads Bissinger. A kind of Hollywood typecast prayer: will Mayor Ed Rendell save the city (the one that allows its retaining wall to collapse)? Probably a couple hundred purchase *Shaving.* Likely fewer read it. But inside I find a pure prayer: "every building, shopper, car and garbage can erupting with the praise and grace of existence, a kind of delirious grief in gratitude for the possibility of existence . . ." The name of this poem is "Burning."

The book is about death. Berg's father and then mother die in the poetry. I read every word inside Robin's Bookstore. I sit on the ratty carpet and read. The city is dying and yet in its death it is most alive. The poet's parents are dying and yet here they are alive. Here is Berg's father three weeks before his death acting as an extra in *Mikey and Nicky,* "implacable mask of a face." May chooses him to walk along the sidewalk, in front of a fleabag hotel, the Royal. The Parker Hotel, at 13th and Locust, wearing a mask, is the Royal. The Parker is a flophouse. Today it's empty, awaiting restoration. Half the windows are lurched open. Part of the old marquee has been uncovered. The old light bulbs are still screwed in. On May's cue, Falk—Mikey—comes along the sidewalk. Nicky's girlfriend tosses a beer bottle out the window of her hotel room. The bottle crashes in front of Falk. The crew sweeps it up. The scene repeats "over and over," pressing invisible imprints in the sidewalk, until deliverance, when May is satisfied.

Writing twenty or twenty-five years after the event, Berg

confuses the name of the film. He thinks it is probably *A New Leaf*. He calls the poem "In *A New Leaf*." But that film, which May releases in 1971, stars Walter Matthau. Berg says the film is about "an alcoholic, her lover, and a stranger who showed up and would, as it happened, try to save her." This describes *Mikey and Nicky* but also *Minnie and Moskowitz*.

Memory, like the city, is subject to points of abandonment.

Minnie lives alone at the Elaine Apartments on Vine Street in Hollywood. She goes on dates with men that don't interest her and walks out on them before the food arrives. She feels, desperately. She hates a sucker, and is one.

Moskowitz is erratic. He throws punches. He launches rocks. He looks like a hippie; he curses like a longshoreman. At the start of the film, in New York, he tells his mother, "I have no future here . . . I got to move." He has to go to the other side.

The L.A. romance of Minnie and Moskowitz lasts four days. "You want to marry me?" They are lying on Minnie's bed. "Yeah, I'll marry you."

Minnie and Moskowitz, young lovers, marry at seventeen in 1881. She can't read. She hasn't gone to school. He has no trade. He can't stand to be a peddler. Something propels him to fight, or flee.

Pogroms begin the year Minnie and Moskowitz marry, more than two hundred of them across the Pale of Settlement. The Czar puts the May Laws into effect the next year. The principal objective is to disconnect Jews from urban life. To limit influence. To limit the accumulation of wealth and its opposite, political organizing against the aristocracy. Anarchists are to blame for the assassination of Alexander II. Jews are to blame for being anarchists.

In 1882 we have to imagine Moskowitz talking to Minnie about the New World.

A few years later, the Czar decrees that only ten percent of Jewish kids can go to secondary school.

There are rumors that Jews will be expelled from Moscow. Carved out like a molten tumor.

They have to decide. First Moskowitz, then Minnie.

The 1900 U.S. Census, filled in by Nathan Weiss, provides the outlines. Julius arrives in the U.S. in 1888, Minnie, and her children Janie (born 1884), Dora (born 1885), and Mary (born 1887), arrive in 1890.

To confirm this sequence, I search for the family record in the census of 1910. A search for both Minnie and Moskowitz returns no results. But it is possible to browse the forms online. The forms follow the path of the enumerator. Up Christian, down 2nd, up Montrose, down 3rd, etc. As I click from one form to the next in succession, I feel I am walking along the sidewalk. Holding the ledger book, I am getting closer to Minnie and Moskowitz.

At the top of each page, the enumerator fills in his name and other pertinent information.

Feuiten.
Feusteau.
Feccolini.
Feustess.

For a while as I walk along with him, I can't tell his name. I can't make it out. I zoom, but that distorts. Then finally, as if deciphering a code, Feinstein. The enumerator is Louis Feinstein.

In April 1910, when the census information is taken, Minnie and Moskowitz reside, still, at 324 Montrose, Ward 2, District 35. Their names appear on sheet 19A, filled in by Feinstein. Moskowitz, age forty-five, tells Feinstein he is a dry goods dealer. This matches the entry in the city directory: "clk," clerk.

After leaving prison in 1892, Julius Moskowitz gives his occupation as tailor (1892, 1894, 1895), laborer (1897, 1898,

1902, 1908), guard (1905), park guard (1909), inspector (1900), and clerk (1907, 1910).

In 1910 four children still live at home: Mary (20), who works as a candy wrapper, Harry (16), Raphael (12), and Dave (8). Minnie says she has given birth nine times. Five children are living. This means that either Dora or Janie is deceased. If Mary is twenty, she is born in 1890, not 1887. Is she born in Russia or America? "Pennsylvania."

Moskowitz's year of immigration? 1882.

This is surely an error.

No year of entry is given for Minnie.

On January 13, 1920, Max Kaplan, the enumerator, comes to the house of Minnie and Moskowitz at 513 Carpenter Street. Kaplan's handwriting is worse than Feinstein's, but I can read his name without difficulty. Now Moskowitz is fifty-five years old. The information Kaplan records is different from the information taken down by Nathan Weiss or Louis Feinstein. Minnie, notes Kaplan, arrives in the United States in 1885, Julius in 1886. Romania substitutes for Russia as country of origin, probably reflecting changing geopolitical boundaries. Perhaps, later in life, Moskowitz feels a newfound connection to his birthplace. Though he won't return.

Mary and Janie ("Jennie") live at home with Harry (24), Raphael (22), and Dave (17). Mary, age twenty-six, is born in Pennsylvania, Kaplan writes. If she is now twenty-six, this means she is born in 1894, not 1887 or 1890. Jennie, now married to a man named Isidore Escourt, from Bucharest, according to further research, is born in 1890 in Romania (and not 1884). But she can't be born in 1890 in Romania if her mother has come to the United States in 1885.

A census is taken every ten years. Before he dies in 1936, Julius, the head of household, and Minnie, his wife, participate in four or five (1890 is missing; we can't know). Every ten years the questions change slightly.

Memory breaks apart.

Family, too, breaks apart.

In 1907, Dora marries a sheet metal worker, Morris Woorman. One year later, she gives birth to a girl, May. The next year, another girl, Bella. Then Dora vanishes from the record.

A woman named Helen, born 1898, replaces her as Morris's wife. May and Bella live with Morris and Helen. But, according to the same census, May lives with her grandparents. Julius and Minnie list May as being part of their household in 1920, suggesting the girl may not be fond of her stepmother.

Dora vanishes, but her daughter is counted twice.

Moskowitz tells the 1900 census taker, Weiss, that he is naturalized in 1892, the year of his imprisonment.

This information doesn't change in 1920. Minnie and Jennie are also naturalized that year, 1892.

If this is true, Moskowitz is released from prison eight months after the March 18 sentencing. This means it is November, with only about six weeks to become a naturalized citizen. What motivates a man to become a citizen of a country that has just forced him to prison on a trumped-up charge? Is it fear? Is it opportunity? Is it the chance of redemption?

43

I SIT ON THE ragged carpet floor of Robin's Bookstore and read *Shaving* by Stephen Berg. Eva is gone. Reginald is gone. They have been for years. I am left in the city, pursuing myself.

"If God existed and could receive us, speak and forgive, would it matter?" I recite the line, from the prose poem "Reading," over and over.

Who can undo what we are? Like an assault—dark street, late, footsteps, something behind you—the world can become fierce ice, no voice, face, or meaning, and you will have to walk through it, seeking the ghost of someone you have loved too much, and can never have.

I get up and ask Larry Robin if Berg ever gives a reading. Gray, great beard, spraying eyes, voracious mouth, Robin devours me as he speaks. "No, no, he won't ever read. He can't stand the attention."

44

In early November, Moskowitz walks out the gate of Moyamensing Prison, turns left, looks down at his feet, and walks up Passyunk Avenue. It is cold and he doesn't have a coat. He crosses Wharton Street along the gate of the Lafayette Cemetery, past the Perseverance Iron Foundry. He negotiates the streetcars and train tracks on Washington Avenue. He barely notices the Catholic cemetery on the corner because, so quickly, he's arrived at Carpenter Street. Moskowitz turns right, walking parallel to Hallowell, Paul, and Ott Streets. The blocks are short, sliced by Clare, Parker, Atherton, and Mechanic Streets. These names will vanish by 1910, a matter of good government. Uniformity devours particularity.

He turns down Young's Court, images of Minnie, Janie, Dora, and Mary crowding his vision. If you dreamed of redemption, Julius, this must be why.

I sit in my silent office tracing Moskowitz's steps on the computer screen.

The maps are silent, too. No street noise, no people.

The buildings are pink or yellow, squares or rectangles. Pink for brick, yellow for wood. The atlas doesn't show the awnings that stretch from the face of every commercial and retail building to the curb's edge. Nor can you see courtyard gates, fire escapes, lampposts, and laundry lines. Nor stoops, usually only two steps high on these impoverished streets, marble slabs. Nor window ledges, nor balconies, nor slate paving stones. Nor signs, in English or Yiddish, nor posters advertising concerts and meetings, nor pushcarts, nor balsam baskets of fruit. Nor horses, pulling delivery carts, nor goats, nor dogs, nor long dresses, filthy aprons, broken shutters, nor wash basins, cellar grates, cobblestones, nor children crowding doorways, sidewalks, peddling, in mothers' arms, on the courtyard floor.

Who is waiting on Young's Court?

Minnie, wife, age twenty-eight.

Janie, daughter, age eight.

Dora, daughter, age seven.

Mary, daughter, age five.

These ages are based on the 1900 census, Dora's only census. The 1900 census is the oldest existing record of the Moskowitz family, and closest to 1892.

A book of old photographs, published in 1983, reveals the lives of the immigrant poor. The photographs, of blacks, Jews, and Italians in ramshackle courtyards and alleys, are analogs to the redlining maps of the 1930s. Children, with filthy faces and hands, wear rough cotton clothing. They have no shoes. In one photograph, a child stands in front of the old Washington Market after it's been torn down, replaced with sickly trees and bushes. He faces east, toward Love of Mercy synagogue. The boy holds a basket. With a heavy coat and a wool cap, he is a peddler. Around the corner, on the graffiti-covered alley where Eva escapes my proposal, a photographer has captured two dozen children. The photograph is taken in summer. The children are looking into the light. Like distant ghosts, they are overexposed.

Even boys held by mothers or sisters wear caps, jauntily

pushed to the side. Boys leave the alley to push carts, strap on baskets, carry bundles. Girls wear frocks, housecoats, and aprons. Girls own the alleys. Girls invent games on the stoop.

Three girls and a mother await Moskowitz. He turns at the coffee roaster and enters the alley. The smell of the coffee roaster brings him to tears.

Janie, eldest daughter, bright, upright, responsible. She is relieved her father is home, but that's one more body to feed, more clothes to wash. No, he is free, and she is glad for her mother. She stands by Minnie when Moskowitz walks in.

She holds Mary. Oldest and youngest, like mother and daughter.

Fierce Dora is missing, I imagine. She is hiding. She is hurt. She can't understand her hurt. She can't understand why she feels betrayed. She has told other girls in the courtyard: My father is dead. She also tells them, as she has heard him say, God is a lie.

In prison, Moskowitz has been told how to become a naturalized citizen. A citizen has dignity. He has standing.

Inside the house, in rooms that are barely boxes with bare blackened plaster on the brick walls, Moskowitz finds none of his anarchist literature. Minnie has burned everything. "Nothing but trouble."

"Not everything," Janie says when they are alone. She hands him the sheets of Most that she has saved.

In my office, I can taste the scene, just as I had felt so close to Moskowitz standing in front of Love of Mercy. The smooth, knowing voice of Janie plays at my lips. The shadow of Dora streaks by.

Janie asks if he has heard about Sasha Berkman, arrested for the attempted murder of Henry Clay Frick. Julius says, yes, in prison we were sometimes allowed to read the news.

Is he a friend of yours?

Is prison cruel, Papa?

Moskowitz wants to tell her it isn't cruel, if you keep to

yourself. But there are immoral people, Janie, desperate people, he wants to say. People who will do anything for a crumb.

He looks at Janie. But where is Dora?

Dora has been telling people you are dead, Papa.

She is angry, that's all.

Stubborn girl, says Minnie later.

His eyes glimmer in the spray of November light.

Months later, the next summer, the economy disintegrates on railroad speculation and a crash in the price of wheat. Emma Goldman, the most charismatic American anarchist and Berkman's former lover, tells a crowd in Union Square, New York, "Demand work; if they do not give you work, demand bread. If they deny you both, take bread. It is your sacred right!" New York police want to arrest Goldman on the same charge that had put away Prenner, Gillis, Jacobs, and Moskowitz: incitement to riot. But Goldman is on her way to Philadelphia.

In the afternoon of the next day, August 23, Goldman meets with a group of Philadelphia anarchists. Short-haired Natasha Notkin, witness in the defense of Moskowitz and the others, makes a memorable impression on Goldman, "the true type of Russian woman revolutionist, with no other interests in life but the movement." Moskowitz doesn't show. A brewing feud between Goldman and Johann Most over Sasha Berkman divides the movement. Most denounces Berkman for the ham-fisted assassination attempt on Frick. Berkman has stolen Most's language, claiming that by trying to kill the anti-union oilman, he is demonstrating Most's idea of "propaganda of the deed." Goldman stays loyal to her former lover. Most tells the *New York Times* that the police shouldn't arrest Goldman, not because he is concerned for her, but because "she is just trying for notoriety and for what she thinks will make her famous."

The split in the movement isn't the reason Moskowitz doesn't show on August 23. The 1900 U.S. Census, recorded by Nathan Weiss, indicates that Minnie gives birth to her first surviving son, Harry, in August 1893. Harry, then, as I have noticed before, is the child of freedom.

At that evening's anarchist meeting, probably at the Radical Library on 8th Street, the group plans for Goldman to headline a mass meeting August 31 at Buffalo Hall. But police arrest Goldman as she tries to slip through the crowd.

Goldman misses H. H. Holmes by less than three months at Moyamensing Prison. She paces her cell awaiting extradition to New York. She asks for something to read. She asks for her mail. The matron says she has no mail, but Goldman knows this is a lie. Someone opens the solid iron door over the square pass-through in her cell door and hands her towels, a needle, and thread. The towels need hemming. No books? The matron brings a bible. "Indignantly, I flung the volume at the matron's feet."

"I had desecrated God's word; I would be put in the dungeon; later on I would burn in hell."

Moskowitz tells Janie that some of the prison guards try to steal your dignity. If you let them, you might as well die.

45

I AM CHASING GHOSTS. This is my thought as I retrace Mosko-witz's walk from Moyamensing Prison. Moskowitz passes two cemeteries. There are several more within a few blocks, some Jewish, some Catholic, a string of three along Washington Avenue for Civil War dead. The atlas maker, in 1895, labels black cemeteries "burying grounds." Ebenezer, Mt. Zion, Mutual. Once, when the city was small and people crowded near the port, they brought their prisoners and their dead out here to the edge of the city. The dead are impure like the prisoners.

Layer the atlas. Development spreads across the screen, pink and yellow. Cemeteries are green. Burying grounds, like lumberyards, are eggshell. New buildings press up to the graves, so close to the dead. Between the living and the dead, who is vanquished? Workers dig up bodies, truck them out. But often the spaces are left blank: a cemetery becomes a square or playground, a field, a patio, the enduring imprint of the dead, ghosts of ghosts.

Myer Wachtel is a milliner at 710 South Street. William Silverstone is a jeweler at 10th and Walnut. German Jews, they are assimilated, wealthy. They purchase a wooded property eleven miles from Wachtel's store, outside city limits, accessible by train and horse-drawn carriage. The property is on a slight hill overlooking a creek. Locals call the area the Black Hills. The earth is stone. Wachtel and Silverstone and their wives, Dora and Julia, purchase the property to establish a cemetery. A rabbi sanctifies the ground.

Wachtel and Silverstone use the cemetery in the 1880s. But for some reason they sell the center portion of the property to the Har Hasetim Association. Har Hasetim: Mount of Olives.

The year is 1893.

Another group, the newly formed Independent Chevra Kadisho, purchases the land on either side of Mount of Olives. Chevra Kadisho: Holy Society.

Independent: open to anyone, regardless of synagogue or homeland association. The society is a collective, to guarantee dignity. "Independent Chevra Kadisho was set up so your family could pay 10 cents a week, or a month, to ensure at death you had a place to be buried. If your family came from a little town in Russia or Romania, you would buy 50 or 100 graves in your own little section."

This is a quote from the *Philadelphia Inquirer*, January 13, 1986. The speaker is Ann Moskowitz, wife of Alan Moskowitz, grandson of Julius.

Moskowitz, says anarchist Joseph Cohen in his memoir, "over time worked his way up to become the trustee of the Jewish burial society."

NATHANIEL POPKIN

46

A SERIES OF CLICKS leads me to a list of the dead. "Independent Chevra Kadisho," it says in modern typeface at the top of the page. Then "Har Jehuda Cemetery." Then "Name," "Last Address," "Age," "Date Buried," "Grave no.," "Line," "Section." I land on this page by following search results for Jennie Escourt, the oldest child of Minnie and Moskowitz, known in childhood as Janie. I puzzle over the list, which is presented, typed, according to the first letter of the deceased's last name. This means that the list, placed inside a book or a binder, has to be regularly updated, retyped to include the latest deceased. We go to great lengths to keep track of ourselves even in death.

This is page one hundred twenty-two. There is no date but that supplied by the computer database, "Pennsylvania and New Jersey, Church and Town Records, 1708–1985." The earliest date someone on the list is buried is January 25, 1907. This is Bella Engelbach of 128 Bainbridge Street. The latest name is Fannie Edelstein, buried May 30, 1947. The information is typewritten, but pen marks lie over the type. Someone, for example, has handwritten Bella's name, in neat, careful print, as if to approximate the typewriter. Someone has written "Sylvia" next to the name of Celia Ellis. Did her friends and family call her Sylvia or had her name been recorded incorrectly? Last names are occasionally crossed out, either with the once customary "x" of the typewriter, or in lines made by hand. Sometimes no name replaces the strike-through, as if the person had been doubly removed. When I get to Minnie and Moskowitz's eldest daughter, Jennie (Janie), I find it almost impossible to read, or comprehend. All I hear is Popkin's voice, "It's no coincidence."

"Escourt Jennie." The "s" and the "c" in "Escourt" are smudged. The machine is imperfect. Age 48, buried May 2, 1934. Grave number 1, line 2-1, section C. This much is simply factual. But then I gasp, turn around, notice a squirrel loosening a yellowing leaf from the plane tree, and snap back to the computer screen, as if electrified. The next line reads:

Last Address: 417 S. 49th Street

47

Just as a city imposes itself on itself, one city imposes itself on the other. There are classical buildings everywhere, with columns, decadent and worn as if they are thousands of years old. One is a bar and club called Revival. I start going there to get away. I go to Revival, Reginald and Eva go to our old bar on 4th Street. Revival is on 3rd Street. The possibility of one city imposes itself on another. It washes over our house like acid. It eats at the joints. We are frayed.

The architectural revival is Greek, not Roman, except in certain cases. The columns are Corinthian. The memory is of early democracy, not empire, but historicism in architecture is a gesture. Interpretation is an open question. It doesn't have to be faithful.

When I walk between the rough columns of Revival, I feel I am rehearsing. I step forward into another world, imagined. I sketch. I drink too much and end up in foreign beds. I forget all about Nicole.

I finish the application for a fellowship in Rome. I stay out of the house. I walk to the city library and study for the last exams.

Eva speaks to me about practical things. She doesn't have enough to pay the gas bill. Can I spot her? She is going to the laundromat. Do I have anything that needs washing? There are dishes in the sink—who has left them? I do the dishes, I pay her bills, I give her clothes to wash. I recognize what I am doing, paying for shame.

48

TAHARA IS THE PRACTICE of purifying the dead. Four anonymous people, the same gender as the deceased, prepare the body for burial. The body is cold. The person is poor: the Independent Chevra Kadisho provides a Jewish burial for people who can't afford a funeral. "Pres., J. Moskovitz, 324 Montrose."

The Independent Chevra Kadisho renovates a set of buildings at 408–412 Christian Street, one-half block from Minnie and Moskowitz's house, in April 1905. The contractor runs behind on the job and his work is shoddy. The Independent Chevra Kadisho refuses to pay.

The new building is to have a room for *tahara*, including a special bath for the dead, and a space for watching over the dead until burial. A person who watches over the dead is called a *shomer*. A *shomer* recites psalms—"The Lord is my shepherd" (Psalm 23), "He will cover you with his feathers and under him you will find refuge" (Psalm 91)—and guards the body until burial to keep evil spirits away.

The new Independent Chevra Kadisho building has a meeting hall and a synagogue for funeral services. Judge John

P. Elkin of the Pennsylvania Supreme Court rules, on April 30, 1906, that the burial society has been wronged. They don't have to pay the contractor.

Mr. Moskowitz, do you believe in a state of future rewards and punishments? (But how can any Jew say yes?)

Specific laws govern the work of *tahara*. The body lies on a table of wooden slats. The four people are silent. They clean the body with simple cloths. They wash the body by pouring water across it, turning the hand and ladle backwards. The dead aren't treated as if they are alive. The four people hoist the body into a bath. In Hebrew a ritual bath is called *mikva*. A *mikva* is also used to cleanse women after menstruation or before marriage.

In the chilled room, members of the Independent Chevra Kadisho dress the body in a white shroud, cinched at the waist, gut, and neck. "Shrouds, of white muslin or linen, are identical for each Jew—symbolizing equality and purity."

The shroud of the man who assaults Moskowitz on Yom Kippur 1889, the shroud of the man who seeks revenge by wrongfully accusing him on October 11, 1891, of passing out fliers with the intent to incite riot, and the shroud of Moskowitz are the same. All Jews are the same in death.

49

Emma Goldman's time in Philadelphia corresponds with the Jewish New Year. August 31, when she is arrested, is the second day of Rosh Hashanah. Her last day in Moyamensing Prison is September 8, Yom Kippur.

On Young's Court, where Moskowitz lives with Minnie, Janie, Dora, and Mary, "children play in filth and garbage."

Emma Goldman takes the stand in New York a month later, October 6, 1893.

> **Assistant District Attorney McIntyre:** Why is it you do not believe in any religion?
>
> **Emma Goldman:** Because I do not think that any church has done a single thing to ameliorate the conditions of the poor.
>
> **McIntyre:** You speak of tyrants here. Whom do you mean by that?
>
> **Goldman:** The Vanderbilts and the Jay Goulds and the representatives of the Government who deprive its working people of food.

That summer, unemployment grows to a million. By the middle of 1894, it is two million. Minnie and Moskowitz take in tailoring. Raphael is born after Harry.

A. Oakley Hall, a former mayor of New York, is Emma Goldman's counsel. He asks her what she means by the term "social revolution."

Goldman: I mean a war between the classes and the masses such as was seen in France in 1871.

Afraid of revolution during economic crisis, police crack down. Does Minnie warn Moskowitz? They are citizens now. Julius can't afford the trouble.

The anarchist movement leaks. Who can stand the conflict? Who can put up with the internecine struggles, Most versus Goldman, Goldman versus Voltairine de Cleyre? Who can risk time in Moyamensing Prison?

De Cleyre, teacher of English, undermines her own cause. "As the years pass and the gradual filtration and absorption of American commercial life goes on," she notices, "my students become successful professionals, the golden mist of enthusiasm vanishes . . ."

In 1892, during the imprisonment of Prenner, Gillis, Jacobs, and Moskowitz, Samuel Gordon, a cigar maker, joins the Knights of Liberty. Gordon is an "ardent disciple" of Johann Most. Voltairine teaches him English; they fall in love. He wants a traditional wife, "exclusive possession, home, children, all that." She refuses the "condition of married slavery."

Paul Avrich is a professor of history in 1977 when he writes *An American Anarchist: The Life of Voltairine de Cleyre*. Avrich notices that de Cleyre bases a fictional story on her relationship with Gordon. Sex is battle. The fictional lovers, says de Cleyre, "hammered away at each after the manner of young radicals with an excess of energy."

De Cleyre's desire for Gordon makes her act the slave. She is caught in her own prison. She gets rid of her cat to appease

Gordon. From her tiny earnings, she pays his medical school tuition. Preaching fierceness and independence in the meeting hall, at home she accedes—until Gordon leaves.

Love from compulsion is no love at all.

But family strains off members of the movement. Family demands attention. Family produces its own need.

The filmmaker Cassavetes hangs a coda on *Minnie and Moskowitz*, after the film ends and the couple get married: in the backyard of a suburban California apartment complex, at picnic tables, at garden tables, children race around with balloons. Minnie and Moskowitz and their mothers—the grandmothers of their children—watch with abandon and self-satisfaction. The camera angle is low and distant; the light is golden. The children hum along as if in a dream.

Cassavetes carries his family life onto the set—figuratively and literally—just as Joseph Cohen carries his daughter into the movement, onto the lap of Voltairine de Cleyre. Starting with Harry, who is born nine months after Julius is released from prison, Julius Moskowitz and Minnie Moskowitz keep making babies. The babies require more space. Julius moves them into a trinity house on another alley (unlabeled on the 1895 atlas) one block west, at 517 Carpenter. They live there for two or three years, after the birth of Harry. For a year, in 1897, they return to their old block of Carpenter, to the other side of the coffee roaster, an alley called Howard Place. Raphael is born the next year, forty feet to the east at 942 S. 4th, on an alley called Hacker Place. Now they are seven at the turn of the century. Julius becomes a watchman. Janie goes to work. Dora, younger, already has. With the extra income, Julius rents 324 Montrose, around the corner. It has a yard for laundry, enough space to take on a boarder. Voltairine calls the upward track "absorption." In London in 1897 she complains to the exiled Russian revolutionary Peter Kropotkin that she can't keep people in the movement. He tells her: "Let them go; we have had the best of them."

50

THE FOUR RADICALS are released from prison in early November 1892, more than a year since their arrest. Weinberg, their comrade, in whose place Gillis had been arrested during the Yom Kippur Ball, recalls in his memoir that Prenner "distanced himself from us right away."

At an evening lecture, years later, the moderator introduces Prenner. Weinberg is in the audience, curious to witness Prenner's transformation. In Weinberg's memory, the moderator employs the same phrase used by Judge Craig Biddle: to make fun, meaning to shame. "For many years he was lost on a path where he made fun of our prophets and God."

Prenner is around the same age as Moskowitz. The two men arrive in the United States about the same time—Prenner in 1886, Moskowitz in 1888. They leave prison the same day. Prenner tells the lecture audience: "I came to America as a child of eighteen. I didn't know the Yiddish language; my entire learning consisted of knowing Russian. I didn't know a thing about our great prophets. I accidentally joined the anarchist party. I threw myself into the movement with my entire passion, into all its activities and struggles."

I must pick up this scrap of Prenner, place it on the frame of the house of Moskowitz. Form emerges.

The immigrant is blind, by nature. He claws for light, one way then the other, to find his way.

Does Moskowitz, with an infant son at home, dress himself in white and enter the synagogue on September 8, 1893, the last day Emma Goldman spends in Moyamensing Prison? The holy day begins with sunset the night before. Purity is written out in dusk. A prayer guides the preparation: *Just as I clothe myself in this white garment, so may You purify my soul and my body, as the prophet Isaiah said, "Even if your sins are like crimson, they will turn snow-white."*

What is it that Moskowitz wants? In a prayer book, I find a poem written by theologian Edward Feld. *God of the faithless and God of the faithful, with doubt, we come in loneliness, we wait silently, we pray expecting nothing, wanting everything.*

The night passes. What does Moskowitz hear? A mantra: *We rebel, we steal, we transgress, we are unkind, we are violent, we are wicked, we are extremists, we yearn to do evil, we are zealous for bad causes.*

Prenner continues, during his lecture, according to Weinberg, "Now my eyes have been opened . . ."

In prison—the part of Moyamensing Prison that the architect, Thomas U. Walter, has modeled on the Temple of Amenhotep III—Emma Goldman recalls, "I had no need of religious lies; I wanted some human book."

After Goldman's arrest, Voltairine de Cleyre takes over for her at Buffalo Hall on August 31. Later, when de Cleyre is ill, Goldman raises money for her care. Goldman rarely wavers in belief; de Cleyre suffers uncertainty. "I have lost my compass; I don't know where I myself stand . . . I don't know anything, anything at all."

Julius, if you attend the evening Yom Kippur service on

September 7, Kol Nidre, do you return the next day? Do you join the annual recitation of the story of Jonah and the whale? Do you fast? Do you put yourself up to judgment? Do you seek mercy? Do you reach for purity? Are you certain of anything? Anything at all?

51

THE PAGES OF the atlas are heavy, as if sogged. First ward, 1905, plate X. Pink for masonry, yellow for wood or "frame," candy colors.

I have found this original atlas in the Urban Archive in the basement of the main library at Temple University. Like the modernist library itself, the hand-drawn lines of the atlas are crisp. The information is scientific: location and size of water mains, sewer lines, height of curbs, dimensions of buildings, width of the street, number of stories.

Julius is cornered. From the time he returns from prison in November 1892, for forty-three years until his death, he moves six times but never leaves this two-square-block neighborhood. The Independent Chevra Kadisho is here, too, at 408 Christian Street. It is labeled "Jewish Church" on the 1905 atlas.

These are landmarks of Julius's world: the John W. Harper Lumber Yard and the Charles Nesbitt Planing Mill, across from the house at 324 Montrose, the Michael Jennings Coal Yard and the Southwark Foundry and Machine Company, the Lit Brothers Department Store stable (for delivery truck horses, presumably), the Emanuel Lutheran German Church. The atlas—an expression of scientific order—doesn't record the tailor shops, delicatessens, shoe stores, peddler stands, butcher shops, restaurants, woolen wholesalers, jewelers, milliners, taprooms, cigar factories, grocers, bakeries, barbershops, or printshops. It doesn't record the benevolent associations, literature societies, collectives, union halls, meeting halls, or holy societies. Like the street lamps and electric poles, streetcar tracks and water pumps, these landmarks have been filtered out.

A map, like time itself, represents distance. As we frame the house of Moskowitz from the scraps of others, it appears one thing happens then the other, in sequence. He is arrested, he repents, he believes. Distance, strangely, condenses. Let's push back, reinstall time. You are a poor tailor, a poor guard, a laborer. You test the synagogue. What do the religious say, the ones you scorn in 1889, the ones who frame you in 1891?

Moskowitz inhabits a tiny house along with Minnie, Janie, Dora, Mary, Harry, Raphael, and David, the same kind of house on each court: three stories, a single room on each floor. No plumbing. One day, Weinberg, who takes it personally every time someone abandons the movement, knocks on the door. How can you abandon the cause after we, loyal to our brothers, have kept your family afloat?

Julius, what do you say?

I don't see it one way or the other. I don't know what is meant by justice.

Look around, Moskowitz! Is this justice?

I don't know what is dignity.

But look at the rags you are wearing.

Come in! Minnie will make you some tea. Sit down and talk.

I've discovered, in my imagination, that standing in the court with Weinberg, Julius, you aren't solemn. You are bright and warm. You like games. The Yom Kippur Ball is a game. You question Weinberg with playful joy.

Julius, your hunger for anarchism is a celebration of people, free from government and religion. You smile at Weinberg. Weinberg sits for tea.

Is there a God, Moskowitz?

Why should I know the answer? You smile back, shrug your shoulders.

You like to joke, like to kid, like to disarm. You like to help. You don't care much for material possessions. You like Weinberg. But there's too much contention, too much sorrow in the movement. There is enough sorrow for a poor man in this world.

And so, Julius, you've repented?

I've decided to look and listen.

Before he leaves, does Weinberg say, "Then the door is always open!"? No, Weinberg has already moved on. "We have had the best of them."

Moskowitz, you don't see it that way. You aren't going anywhere.

To struggle for holiness, goodness, justice requires a man to stay.

I have discovered fragments of a search, for holiness, perhaps: the founding of a cemetery, Har Jehuda, around 1895, for the proper burial of Jews; the founding of the Independent Chevra Kadisho, which will bury the indigent first at Har Hasetim and then, when that proves impossible, at Har Jehuda; the founding, along with other secular and religious Jews, of an organization called the Sons of Jacob and, soon afterward, the hosting of a citywide conference to raise money to alleviate the suffering of victims of pogroms; the building of the new Independent Chevra Kadisho to extend its free burial service to more immigrants that same year, 1905; the decision not to abandon Har Hasetim despite the insolvency of the original owner and the hard, impenetrable rock beneath the surface of the land of the Black Hills, and to manage it into perpetuity.

Do all these actions make up for the tearing out of the heart?

If I attach these fragments to the frame I've already assembled—we may call it a tabernacle—I have fashioned the structure of a life, one that eschews clear answers, that muffles doctrine. Eva would be enthralled.

I walk downtown. I walk to the site of the Yom Kippur protest and then to the hall, at 512 S. 3rd Street. I try to walk on the shady side of the street. I'm reminded of the intimacy. Three people are enough to fill the sidewalk. The buildings try to swallow the street. A man like Moskowitz, an immigrant, has to swallow the aggression. Or push back. I walk down 3rd Street to Christian. I want to see the Independent Chevra Kadisho at 408–412 Christian Street. I want to walk from there to 324 Montrose or from there to 513 Carpenter. If I can collide with you, Moskowitz, I will feel, at least for a fleeting second, how you experience a search for meaning. I will feel the sun, the same sun, and I will sense the buildings around me like a shroud. Perhaps, then, I will have an answer.

But none of this is possible because nothing is left of Julius's world.

The site of the Independent Chevra Kadisho, its offices, its room for the ritual preparation for the dead, the social hall, and the school, is the edge of a bland public housing development, itself the replacement for a project, Southwark Plaza, first completed in 1962. 408–412 Christian Street consists of three short attached town houses in an eight-house row behind clipped bushes and small patches of grass. The network of alleys between 3rd and 4th, 4th and 5th Streets, along with Montrose and Carpenter, Kimball, League, and Hall Streets, has been erased. I approximate the position of 324 Montrose and 942 S. 4th Street, and I find myself gazing into open lawn, concrete sidewalks, aluminum downspouts. A fence keeps me from finding the position of 429 Carpenter. I walk stupidly in the manufactured emptiness.

The row of buildings across from the Independent Chevra Kadisho, dating to the Civil War: that too has been erased, for a parking lot attached to the Settlement Music School. The corner opposite remains as it was, a three-story store-front with an iron post and a string of curved brick up the corner. At the approximate site of 324 Montrose, I gaze out, as if I can see through a rear window of the Moskowitz house, at the steeple of the Emanuel Lutheran German Church. From my position inside the housing development, I can't tell that a group of Vietnamese immigrants have converted the church into a Buddhist temple. I can't see the ten-foot statuary or the golden door.

Minnie and Moskowitz move to 513 Carpenter around 1910. Their house is gone, along with 517, where they had re-sided before in the rear alley. Someone has put up a new row of houses, meaningless buildings on a butchered block.

But isn't there a single trace? In a box in the Urban Archive I find a sheet of slide photographs of Julius's neighborhood from 1960. The first slide shows a residential street, possi-bly Carpenter or Montrose. The marble stoops have been scrubbed. Petunias grow in flower boxes. Below the slide, an-other shows a wrecking ball, a half-demolished building with exposed interior plaster walls, and, in the foreground, a single window, all that's left of the front wall. To the right is a dark photo of a rundown building with its windows sealed with sheet metal. Below that is another half-demolished house, its floral wallpaper exposed. A sign says, "Arrow Wrecking Company Demolition Engineers." Another slide shows some buildings on an alley. Could this be Howard Place or Young's Court or Hacker Place? The windows of these lost houses are broken. The plaster is hacked apart, the ground rising with debris and dust, as, in the reverse of the neighborhood only a generation before, it is about to swallow the broken, weakened buildings. The sixth slide on the sheet: "Looking east at the 300 block of League—now demolished."

I have seen other photos of Moskowitz's neighborhood in this period. In one, the houses and stores, including an Abbot's Dairy Luncheonette across from Howard Place, are boarded up, awaiting demolition. In another, taken April 17, 1958, street workers are repaving the 400 block of Christian Street. The photograph has been ripped apart and taped back together. The tape bubbles like a network of streams, or like gathering smoke before the surge of fire. The Independent Chevra Kadisho is in the left of the photograph. The western part of the building, added in 1905 by the incompetent contractor, has been punched away. In one year more the entire block will have vanished.

The archivist brings me another box, "Southwark Plaza." Inside is a series of eight by ten glossy black-and-white prints in plastic sheets—photographs of models of the housing project that replaces Moskowitz's neighborhood, produced by the architects Stonorov and Haws. The first is the grand view, as if from the sky, of three twenty-six-story towers, and a network of low-rise buildings and courtyards. Surrounding neighborhoods are put back in order. Trees are planted. Traffic is light. The model is intricate but also heroic, and therefore an architectural lie. Clouds have parted. Everything is bathed in new light.

Renderings follow the photographs of the model. Here is the church facing one of the towers, with an elegant public plaza in between. Here are a mother pushing a stroller and a boy holding a balloon in one of the low-rise courtyards. The leaves of the tall trees are blotted as in the work of a Japanese court painter. Here a man approaches the arcade of one of the towers. Here a woman reads the newspaper. Here, in a black-and-white photograph in the same sequence, the towers rise along 4th Street. Contractor signs clutter the corner. There is no trace of Minnie and Moskowitz. It is winter 1961.

In another box I discover a slide: "Last building demolished, S.E. Cn. 4th and Carpenter." This is written in pencil below the slide. Above the slide: "Looking south on 4th St at Carpenter."

The building in the photograph is a typical corner storefront from Moskowitz's time, with bay windows, an iron column, and a decorative cornice above the store window. The southeast corner of 4th and Carpenter, catercorner from the trinity house at 942 rear S. 4th Street, where Raphael Moskowitz is born, is, however, the Emanuel Lutheran German Church. I look again at the slide. I can't make out the street sign or the street names on either side of the cornice above the door. It is like looking into fog. But this time I notice that the photographer has written "(?)" after the word "at" and then later, overriding it, "Carpenter," a stab in the dark.

Erasure triggers amnesia, as if the demolition of the neighborhood obliterates memory, too.

52

THE WHITE PAINTED ROOM I move into in June 1991 is above a barbershop. The barber tells stories of World War II, the Pacific front. He says he will never forget the fragrant smell of the bushes and the sand. He returns home postwar and settles in a modern neighborhood called New Eastwick. New Eastwick replaces Eastwick, a cluttering of old village houses and farm shacks. I tell him I've never been there. "It isn't much to see," he says.

"You were only in the Pacific?"

"No, not at first. At first I was stationed in Rome."

"Rome," I say, "I had hoped to go to Rome . . ."

I never hear from anyone connected with the fellowship. I never call or write to inquire.

I bring my new haircut to our bar. Reginald calls and tells me to come. "One last time," he says. The bar is filled with our friends. I sit in the front, in the window. Eva and Reginald come in. I stay in my seat. Reginald stops in front of me—my oldest college friend. Eva stands behind. Reginald lights a cigarette. The night pours into the narrow room. Eva steps away, into the black. She drifts to the back room. I don't remember when Reginald follows. He is there and then he is gone.

53

FOR YEARS, BLOCKING OUT our life at 417 S. 49th Street, I fail to look for them, Reginald and Eva. I forget that they, too, are living adults. I enroll in a graduate program in architecture. I travel. I become a star associate in a medium-sized firm. I get recognized in the architecture press for the interior design of a children's hospital pavilion. I marry. I move away for a new position. I return to work in a large firm that designs museums, civic buildings, and university dormitories. I tell everyone I want to build big. I want to have an impact. I have to find a way to be remembered. I buy a house on a bourgeois street. Facing south and raised up on a terrace, the house has sunlight dancing inside. I divorce. I go out on my own.

For years I forget. I work constantly. Julius gathers in, I push everyone away. We don't have kids, Laura and I. We tell ourselves we don't want them. This is a lie. When we divorce there's almost nothing to split up.

Reginald? Eva? The Internet offers search boxes everywhere, but I never search. I don't even type their names. Flushed by shame for abandoning the people I have loved so much, for isolating myself, I block out Eva's humiliation.

Julius, it occurs to me, you are never afraid. Not of the religious, not of the jailer, not of the opinions of Weinberg or Cohen. Not of yourself, for turning. Not of death.

I force myself to forget about what happened in Eva's room in May 1991. I let myself be fractured. Even so many years later, I won't be vulnerable enough to press "Search."

And then, nearly three weeks after I discover that Jennie Escourt too had lived (without any children of her own), and died, at 417 S. 49th Street, the letter comes, a real letter, on paper.

The handwriting on the envelope is familiar. I've see fragments of it in the margins of Kierkegaard.

The letter is from Eva.

Dear Nicholas.

For a long time I thought I should write or call or something, but after a while that seemed ridiculous. I always could take care of things myself. Anyway, what was the point? Even after your son was born and Reginald went off wherever, I thought I should, but then I didn't. I told myself you didn't deserve to know.

I named him Jonah, Nicholas, I don't know why, but that's the name I chose. I always liked that story, Jonah and the Whale. Jonah died last week, that's why I am writing. Is this a terrible stab in the back? He knew who you were, Nicholas, because finally I told him. I am sure he had started to search for you, but he was slow to get around to things he really should have been doing. He really was his own person, Nicholas, he had his way, ever since he was little. I could only suggest and I learned to. I thought I had figured it out.

He died crossing a street. The streets here in Washington are dangerous—they're so wide and no one slows down. No one slows down for anything here. I have a terrible need to see you now. I didn't feel that need when I sat down to write. I didn't feel anything, that's the only way I could do it in the first place. My hand as it writes, the ink, I don't know, one hardly writes like this anymore, is loosening things. I am sorry. I must stop. My address is on the envelope. You can see that, I don't need to say.

Eva

54

I SIT ON MY STOOP, early morning, Eva's letter is folded in my pocket. The row houses on my side of the street are stacked on high ground. The stoop itself is five steps up. From here, from time to time, I watch starlings and finches float in and out of the cherry trees.

The block is quiet. Where are the ball players? Are they back in school already? With Reginald, years ago, I learn to sit on the stoop, which we share with our neighbors. In those days you might find a remnant of the city before suburban flight, someone who has spent his entire working life in a factory. A man exists in my memory, emaciated face, graveyard of teeth, arthritic dog. The breath of the dog, inescapable at the height of the stoop, tastes of death. Then one day neither the man nor his dog appears for a walk.

For days, I rehearse imaginary conversations. I get up, get in the car, and head to Washington, only to turn around.

My son, a real person. I want to know him, but that's most impossible of all. I find Eva's number, but I can't call. I start to write and stop, in a daze. No, I must write. She's asked that I write. She's given me her address.

Someone I don't know has died; that part of me is gone.

Why, Eva? I ask this over and over. I want to know how it is I could never be trusted to know.

Was it cruel of her? Is this cruelty different from mine? The cruelty of making her need me, the cruelty of rejection, the cruelty of my silence.

The walls of the tabernacle are leveled.

I search for what's solid. My house, at 2537 Aspen Street, is the last in the row, up against the corner store, now a sushi restaurant. Green tea and seaweed salad are always available.

I look up and there is the bus, white, with red and blue accents, dumping particulates on my corner.

The bus is always in earnest.

"Moskowitz!" The laconic voice of Popkin. He's gotten off the bus. "I didn't know you lived here."

We exchange pleasantries. His glasses are a little steamed from the humidity.

He is going to ask about the parking lot on Bainbridge Street, if he remembers.

"What are you doing on my block?"

He tries to wipe the steam off his glasses, puts them back on, looks up at the sky, removes them again. Squints.

"Coffee with a friend. I never see him in summer and—"

"Now it's fall."

"Just about. What's happening with the project—" he asks, as if reaching for a memory. "The parking lot."

"Gone. I lost it."

"What do you mean you lost it?"

"I couldn't do it. You're free to keep dreaming the lot."

"This is why you don't look too good?"

"Maybe."

"Too bad! I was looking forward to seeing what you would build."

"—"

"You really aren't all right."

"Memories. I guess you remind me of college, 49th Street. You were in love with Abigail," I say, aware of what I'm doing, pushing the conversation toward Eva.

"Well . . . it wasn't anything like you and Eva."

"I'm sorry we all had to go through that—"

"What?"

"The torment, the drama."

"We were young."

"—"

"I haven't seen Abigail since we graduated."

"You didn't—"

"No, she went right back to the West Coast."

The letter is out of my pocket, soft in the hand like a dog's ear. My hand shakes. "I haven't asked. You still work at the hotel? It's been so long. That's probably a ridiculous question."

"But I do! They put up with me leaving poems for the guests."

"You don't!"

"No, I don't," he says, his face collapsing in.

"Eva—"

"What about Eva?"

"She had a kid, Popkin. She had a kid and raised him—my kid. I never met him. I never knew about him. He was an adult, older than we were . . . this says he got hit by a car."

55

"WHAT AM I DOING at present? I begin from the beginning and then I begin backwards." I mark the passage in blue ink while sitting in the office at the table used once in my mother's family bakery in Holland. It's from a section of *Repetition*, "Letters from a Young Man," written by the poet.

Eva says she isn't ready for me to come to Washington. But she will come here in two weeks—her idea. She wants to talk in person, "see your life," she says. I picture an examination room. I want to learn about my son. I haven't mentioned the house at 417 S. 49th Street.

Do I take her there? I try to imagine us, together, searching for her lost room. But how can I?

And how do I mount toward contrition?

What is the shape of repentance?

I have to begin rebuilding somehow. Jonah's death has forced my hand.

So I begin backwards, sitting in a realtor's glum office on Baltimore Avenue. Nadia has the checkbook in hand. I sign the documents, an agreement to purchase the house at 417 S. 49th Street. The young realtor eyes Nadia.

The day before the appointment in the realtor's office, I tell Nadia that I am the client interested in the house. "I'm going to conduct some architectural experiments," I say. I tell her that when I lived there from 1989 to 1991 much of the original woodwork, cabinetry, and details still remained, breathing in the same air they always had, just as on April 30, 1934, when Minnie and Moskowitz sat at the dining room table waiting for the doctor to come downstairs to tell them that their oldest child, the child they once called Janie, had died. I describe Julius Moskowitz standing on Bainbridge Street in front of the Love of Mercy synagogue goading the religious to betray themselves. I tell her how I have imagined that Janie was loyal to her father despite the eight months in jail that followed his arrest on October 11, 1891. She hid away his secret documents.

The lights in the office are out—it is late afternoon, and we rely on the sharpening sun. I watch it slide across her face, revealing, in this light, the rich cinnamon of her eyes.

I share my vision for the house: the experiment is about time, about bodies past and present. This is a chance for me to begin, quietly, slowly, to become a man again. Then, later, perhaps, an architect. The architecture of the room, in my vision, will appear the same as it did in 1934. I hesitate and then correct myself. "Not spring of 1934. Fall, let's say, of 1933. Before she becomes ill, Janie, now Jennie, often walks to Baltimore Avenue to take the trolley to City Hall and then the subway to Lombard-South. This gives her a chance to window-shop on South Street, and, if she can afford it, pick up something nice for Minnie and Moskowitz on her way to their house at 513 Carpenter. She will walk down South Street to 6th, past the copper onion domes of the B'Nai Reuben Synagogue, where she attends services when she can. She will cross Christian Street just west of the Independent Chevra Kadisho, where someone, a *shomer* she is called, sits with someone else who has died. At Carpenter, feet aching,

NATHANIEL POPKIN

she turns left." The rest of the house, I say to Nadia, the furniture, the wall coverings, the art, these will appear as I recollect them, circa 1990.

"And there is a living layer, right?" she asks, prescient as usual, but before I can answer she has gotten up to collect the papers for the settlement. I wrench myself to follow her back and forth to the copy machine, but after a while I desist.

56

"JULIUS MOSKOWITZ, a Russian-Jew and president of the Independent Chevra Kadisho on 408 Christian Street in South Philadelphia, decided to create a burial ground for East European Jews without regard to country of origin in the mid-1890s." I take this from a book called *The Jewish Community of South Philadelphia.*

The cemetery office is in a two-story simple stone building Julius builds in 1923. I decide to drive there. I bring Nadia along. Afterwards, I suggest we go for crêpes at Beau Monde, "across from B'Nai Reuben Synagogue . . . stripped of its letters and its stars." But Nadia doesn't respond.

"We'll have lunch after?" I suggest.

"Lunch after cemetery," she says, in a distant voice, as if repeating.

"Yes?"

"No, no, I don't want crêpes. And anyway, I can't. I have . . ." She trails off and I look at her, staring forward at the road.

"You have . . ." But I stop myself; I don't need to hear. I have no work for her, even if I do have enough money to keep paying her for a while. In Paris she has cut her hair, on

220

an angle at the neckline, a French style. She stares out from beneath her new haircut; it is still Nadia, lips more sensual than Eva's (which were sometimes chapped in the northeastern winter she wasn't used to). She runs her hand over the sharp edge of the French cut above the ear. Something about this movement—a nervous gesture?—tells me I won't see her much after this.

I try to ignore this thought as we cross the city line into Upper Darby.

"It's not bad here," she says idly.

"No, not at all . . . You're going to help me find Julius," I say. "That's good." And I smile with gratitude.

The stone building has an office and an apartment for the cemetery caretaker. The windows are small. It is cool inside against the Indian summer heat.

I think of Dora, who disappears from the Internet record before the 1910 census. Dora and Jonah, somehow I've come to merge them together, perhaps because they both died too soon. Inside the cemetery gate we walk in loops up and down lanes of the dead, eyes fatiguing, seeking her name. The wind blows hard against our faces. We don't find her marker. I ask the manager if he can help us. The cemetery record may be all there is. In the office the manager flips through leather-bound books and old index cards. I look around. There is a portrait of Julius's first son, Harry Moskowitz, in shirt and tie, sitting in a winged armchair. A handsome, dark-haired, middle-class man, with rabbit's-foot eyebrows. We might imagine that Harry, the freedom child, is Julius's talisman. For years they work together here at Har Jehuda and at the Chevra Kadisho on Christian Street, arranging dignified ends.

Close by Harry: here, at long last, is Julius, his bust as a bas-relief in molded copper, as if in flesh.

Erected By The
Independent Chevra Kadisho

In Loving Memory Of
Julius Moskowitz
Founder Of The Har Jehuda Cemetery
Who Served Faithfully As President Of
The Independent Chevra Kadisho For
Thirty-Seven Years

Julius has great jowls and a mustache—a Steppe face oddly reminiscent of Stalin. In the copper bust Moskowitz wears a skullcap on top of thick, carefully combed hair, a tie and jacket, and the far-seeking warm eyes of a caretaker father. I recall my imagined story of Julius's return to Carpenter Street, to the courtyard behind the coffee roaster, a return to family. I recall his secret connection to Dora, the girl who lashes out. I recall Janie's loyalty, handing her father the tracts she had found and saved.

The portrait of Harry makes me think of another son of a radical, the child of Voltairine de Cleyre, also named Harry, born around the same time as Mary, the third daughter of Minnie and Moskowitz. "For the young mother, however, it was not a happy occasion," writes the historian Paul Avrich in his *An American Anarchist*. Voltairine leaves Harry for a year to go lecture for the Women's National Liberal Union. "She had things she wanted to do with her life, and he was not part of them."

Children complicate the radical life.

Yet must we think of Voltairine as a bad mother?

Second daughter Dora means to live her own way. According to the few available records, she is the first of Minnie and Moskowitz's daughters to work, the first to marry. But marriage—isn't it a kind of trap? Dora goes to live with her husband Morris's family at 435 Carpenter, adjacent to the old courtyard next to the coffee roaster. She hasn't gone far. Dora gives birth to May, a daughter, March 31, 1908; public records I find on the Internet reveal that eighteen months later, on

September 27, 1909, at age twenty-two, she delivers another girl, Bella. Two weeks later, Dora, dressmaker at age fourteen, is dead, complications of childbirth.

Moskowitz gathers—in death he brings them in. "The Independent Chevra Kadisho was established to afford free burial in cases where the family of the deceased is too poor to bear the expense."

I look back at the photograph I've taken of the bust of Moskowitz: great heavy eyes like sacs—eyes of worry and yet eyes alight.

A placard hangs in the corner of the cemetery office. "Independent Chevra Kadisho In Memory Of Our Departed Officers And Directors." Moskowitz is listed first. "Jehuda Moskowitz, Pres." Jehuda: Jew.

57

For weeks I have been seeking Julius, and seeking myself. Now the manager points us in the right direction, and the Moskowitz family comes alive, as if gathered during a lawn party to celebrate a wedding or a birthday: Minnie ("Beloved Mother") and Moskowitz ("Beloved Father") in the second row, C section. To their right: Harry and his wife, Sarah, and next to Harry, David and his wife, Anne. Behind David is his older brother Ralph (Raphael) and his wife, Eva. Mary, the last of Minnie and Moskowitz's children born in Romania (or Russia), according to the 1900 census, is to the left of Ralph with her husband, Herman. Jennie (Janie) is next to her younger sister Mary. "At Rest," it says on Jennie's grave. Died April 30, 1934, aged 48 years, childless.

We can see Julius's shaken hand on her death certificate, upright careful script of another age. He will arrange her burial. He has done it before.

One year and two months later, Minnie dies. And nine months after Minnie: Moskowitz. Jennie's grave is set back slightly as if to allow room for her husband, Isidore Escourt, but Isidore remarries and is interred with his second wife, Anne.

Dora, second daughter, ferocious and willful, dies well before Julius sets aside this spot for his family. He situates her grave alongside the office wall. Nadia places a flower—I don't even realize she has it—on top of Dora's grave. Morris, her husband, inscribes the slender monument, "In memory of my beloved wife."

Only later, when Julius begins organizing a family plot, does it become apparent: Dora is separated from everyone. There are hundreds of lives in between.

ACKNOWLEDGMENTS

The members of the Working Writers Group brought this book along: Ann de Forest, Louis Greenstein, Mark Lyons, David Sanders, Debra Leigh Scott, and particularly Miriam Seidel, who designed the dust jacket, and publisher Douglas Gordon, who did everything else to turn the manuscript into a book. Rivendell Writers Colony and the Athenaeum of Philadelphia offered space and support, and the Athenaeum generously provided the image plate from the 1895 Bromley Atlas. Avi Winokur guided me through the moral landscape of Yom Kippur. Liz Spikol, Peter Siskind, Kate Oxx, Anders Uhl, Libby Mosier, Christine Neulieb, Linda Gallant-Moore, Joan Popkin, and Leah Paulos read and offered guidance. Rona Buchalter gave me her unlimited faith and eyes for finding the way.